*Between*
Midnight *and* Dawn

## Praise for *Light Upon Light: A Literary Guide to Prayer for Advent, Christmas, and Epiphany*

"Maybe it's not right to think of feasting during the somewhat penitential season of Advent, but that is what this book is: a rich feast."—LAUREN F. WINNER, author of *Girl Meets God* and *Still*

"In our individual darknesses we long for more light. Sarah Arthur understands this, and, as if pulling together scores of candles with burning wicks, she illuminates our whole year with the gift of flaming words. A treasure of enlightenment."—LUCI SHAW, poet and author of *Breath for the Bones* and *Adventure of Ascent*

"An elegant and accessible gem for the literature lover to focus, meditate, and celebrate this time of year, providing a fresh view of what the birth of Christ means to a shattered and fragile world."
—JILL PELÁEZ BAUMGAERTNER, poet; Professor of English and Dean of Humanities and Theological Studies, Wheaton College

"A beautifully navigated journey through a treasury of literary wisdom—a book to cherish."—JEREMY BEGBIE, Professor of Theology and director of Duke University Initiatives in Theology and the Arts

"Arthur's curation is sensitive and inviting to epiphany . . . in short: both spiritual succor and pure pleasure." —*Image* journal

"It will quiet your heart and bring balm to your soul in the midst of a ridiculously busy time of the year." —JoHANNAH REARDON for *Christianity Today*

"Part of the joy of *Light Upon Light* . . . is discovering the texts Arthur has chosen to be in conversation with one another, and with scripture readings." —NATHANIEL LEE HANSEN for *The Cresset*

"*Light Upon Light* is for all lovers of a word well spoken. It is for the pilgrim, the sojourner; for those who desire to journey toward Bethlehem rather than to march. And who believe, like Sarah Arthur, that there is eternal power in great literature, power to pierce the darkness with its Spirit-infused light."
—Shari Dragovich for *The Englewood Review of Books*

# Between
# Midnight *and* Dawn

*A Literary Guide to Prayer for
Lent, Holy Week, and Eastertide*

Compiled by Sarah Arthur

PARACLETE PRESS
BREWSTER, MASSACHUSETTS

2016 First printing

*Between Midnight and Dawn: A Literary Guide to Prayer for Lent, Holy Week, and Eastertide*

Copyright © 2016 by Sarah Arthur

ISBN 978-1-61261-663-6

Library of Congress Cataloging-in-Publication Data:
Arthur, Sarah.
  Between midnight and dawn : a literary guide to prayer for Lent, Holy Week, and Eastertide / compiled by Sarah Arthur.
     pages cm
  Includes bibliographical references and index.
  ISBN 978-1-61261-663-6
  1. Lent—Prayers and devotions. 2. Eastertide—Prayers and devotions. I. Title.
  BV85.A78 2015
  242ʾ.34—dc23                              2015032228


10 9 8 7 6 5 4 3 2 1

Published by Paraclete Press
Brewster, Massachusetts
www.paracletepress.com


Printed in the United States of America

For my husband, Tom,
whose companionship during the darkest hours
helps me turn with hope
toward the promised sunrise.

*. . . Between midnight and dawn, when the past is all deception,*
*The future futureless, before the morning watch*
*When time stops and time is never ending;*
*And the ground swell, that is and was from the beginning,*
*Clangs*
*The bell.*

— T. S. ELIOT, from "The Dry Salvages" in *Four Quartets*

# CONTENTS

Welcome to this literary guide to prayer for the seasons of Lent, Holy Week, and Eastertide. With this book we have completed the liturgical year, which began (rather backwards) with *At the Still Point: A Literary Guide to Prayer in Ordinary Time*, a collection of poetry and fiction for the longest liturgical season, running from Pentecost to Advent. We followed that with *Light Upon Light: A Literary Guide to Prayer for Advent, Christmas, and Epiphany*, which includes readings to accompany our journey through the wintry darkness.

If you already have encountered one or both of the other collections, you will recognize the same format and spirit here. If not, no worries: each collection stands alone, with its own unique curation of voices and themes. In any case, you have entered what you might think of as a quiet library: a company of books, of readers, of writers, welcoming you in. Make yourself at home.

With this book we arrive at Lent, those forty days (not including Sundays) leading up to Easter. It's that time when the church—and the soul—faces the tomb, aware of its own mortality, seeking the promise of light on the other side. It's a journey we make alone, yet not alone, surrounded as we are by those who have caught a glimpse of sunrise. And we need them.

Whoever has lain awake during moonless hours between midnight and dawn knows this: the darkness is final. It owns the earth utterly. It takes hold in the tick of the clock and the stillness of the woods and the shallow breath of your own mute body. Anyone taking notes during those hours would be convinced there is nothing more: no further turning of the earth, no future flourishing of existence under a warm star, no life recalled from the tomb. It is the last and definitive night.

But then, by some magic that cannot be quantified, it is not. The earth stirs, inhales, stretches. A bird pipes in a forsythia, as if talking in its sleep, startled awake by its own daring. Light, where there was no light, makes visible: first the outline of a window, then the edge of the bed, your own hand, a book open on the covers.

There's no saying precisely when the turn happens. But it does. Every morning. From the beginning of the world.

It's the same miracle of awakening that happens when winter changes to spring. The earth, frozen in a silence that will not break, the days brief and brutal, our own cold selves making their grim way through the dark . . . and then . . . and then . . . something shifts. Light in the east, earlier than we remembered; a lift in the air, like a warm updraft; a patch of mud that grows and grows as the snow recedes.

It's the same turning as when the church, emptied of vestments and cold as a crypt, lights one candle. When the community finds itself, against all odds, redeemed. Lenten sorrow makes way for Easter joy, and nothing—nothing—will quench the dawn.

And it's the same shift that happens when the soul, alone in grief or guilt or illness or isolation, finds company in the life-giving words of another. During the midnight hours we shelter our guttering faith, and by its light we read poetry and prose that transcend centuries, hemispheres. Words from poets whose battles with God do not lead to victory but to a kind of grumpy determination. Stories from novelists who have tumbled into the abyss of their own undoing—of everyone's undoing—and found Someone there already, holding the bottom rung of the rescue ladder. *Raise your eyes*, these voices say. *Look to the east. Do you not see it? There. The dawn.*

In this collection you will find such voices. And their words are not always easy. Lent is, after all, the season of repentance, of soul-searching, of Christ's lonely journey to the Cross. We start in darkness together, naming its various shades, uncertain, even, that morning will come. And the night deepens, if possible, during Holy

Week, when the crowds that once celebrated hope's arrival now spurn it with venom, taking all of humanity down in the process. The stone is rolled across the cold tomb; and there we are, buried with Jesus, left with nothing but a body wound in a white sheet, destined for dust.

But take heart, these voices say. There is a power here in the bowels of the earth, a "deeper magic," as C. S. Lewis called it.[1] Death is not given the final word. In the night of the tomb, our Lord sits up, shakes off the sheet, swings his feet down onto the cold stone floor. He steps out from the crypt into the cool of a damp garden, inhales, smiles. Christ doesn't need to turn east to greet the sunrise: he is himself the Dawn by whose "light we see light" (Psalm 36:9). The sun will not set again. That was our last night. Ever.

So, at last, we enter the season of Eastertide, which runs from Easter Monday to Pentecost. We step into the morning of a new day. These poets and novelists remind us that the sunrise is undeserved, but here we are. Our battles are ongoing but just skirmishes, really, the last desperate attempts of the losing side to go down fighting. The war itself is over. When it's our time to physically enter the tomb of our own mortality, we know that if we have been buried with Christ, we will rise with Christ. We'll ride on his coattails, so to speak. And what we'll see then won't be simply light at the end of a tunnel, but light at the end of all things, the final and permanent morning.

So let it begin.

## HOW TO USE THIS BOOK

This guide to prayer is divided into twenty-one sections: six for the season of Lent, beginning with Ash Wednesday; eight for Holy Week and the Triduum (the three holy days of Good Friday, Holy

Saturday, and Easter itself); and seven for Eastertide, or the seven weeks following Easter (also known as the Great Fifty Days). Each section begins with a suggested outline for daily prayer, including an opening prayer (often taken from classic poetry), a psalm for the day or week, suggested Scriptures, five to seven literary readings, an opportunity for personal prayer and reflection, and a closing prayer (again, generally taken from classic poetry). As with *At the Still Point* and *Light Upon Light*, a theme for each section provides an organizing thought that holds it all together.

Begin your time of devotion each day or week with the opening prayer; then move on to the suggested psalm. It can be meditated upon daily, or you may wish to read only a portion of the psalm each day. Or find a particular section of the psalm with which you especially resonate and dwell there awhile, meditating on the words as a kind of personal prayer. The psalms as Hebrew poetry are some of the greatest literature you will encounter, providing echoes and resonances that a mere cursory skim will miss.

After the psalm, the rest of the Scriptures as well as the readings can be read daily or spread throughout the week as a guide for prayerful reflection. As you may already have discovered, the medium of poetry lends itself rather well to this kind of meditation. It is nearly impossible to read a poem both quickly and well. Often we find ourselves reading it a second or even a third time, savoring its images, marveling at the crafted word patterns. It may not be all that difficult to imagine how to turn your poetic meditation into prayerful reflection, inviting God into your wonderings and insights. With the fiction excerpts, however, in many cases you will be jumping in mid-story, with only a brief editor's note to orient you to people, places, and plot. It may take you a moment to settle in to the author's voice, to let the story weave its spell on your imagination.

That's why some of the excerpts are rather long, because fiction doesn't work its magic right away. You might consider picking a day in the week in which you will focus only on the story rather than trying to cram the other readings in as well. Meanwhile, you are absolved from trying to hunt for the story's "point." Some of the fiction may have obvious connections to the section's theme; others may not. Rather than agonize over an excerpt, it is perfectly okay to move on, trusting that if the Spirit has something to say to you (whether it has to do with the theme or not) the insight will come in time.

Once you have done the readings, there is an opportunity for personal prayer and reflection, whether through silence or journaling or whatever mode works for you (see the discussion of *lectio divina*, below, for more ideas). What jumped out at you from the readings? When did you sense God's presence? What might God be saying to you?

Finally, wrap up your time with the closing prayer.

Still unsure of how to engage fiction or poetry prayerfully? Consider applying aspects of the practice of *lectio divina* (divine reading) to this process. It is an ancient method for prayerful meditation on the Scriptures, involving four steps: *lectio* (reading the passage), *meditatio* (meditating; reading it over several more times slowly), *oratio* (letting the text speak to you by paying attention to words, phrases, images, or ideas), and *contemplatio* (shifting one's focus to God; resting in God's presence). To be clear, I recognize that these literary readings are not the words of Scripture. But the basic principles of *lectio* that one might apply to Scripture can be applied to novels and poetry—since Scripture is, among other things, great literature.

We have already mentioned the opportunity for personal prayer and reflection that follows the readings. This is the *oratio* and *contemplatio* stage. You have read the passage (*lectio*)—perhaps several times, slowly (*meditatio*)—and now you go back through it, making note of the words, phrases, images, metaphors, or ideas that "shimmer." What jumps out at you? What speaks to you (*oratio*)? You may even want to write it down. Then invite God to show you why this word or phrase spoke so strongly. What is God up to? In what ways do you sense God's presence in the midst of this reading? Finally, pause and simply rest in that presence (*contemplatio*). There are no demands on you in this moment. You are simply resting in God.

Wait for the dawn.

It's coming.

# ASH WEDNESDAY

## *Wearing Mortality*

OPENING PRAYER

In thy word, Lord, is my trust,
To thy mercies fast I fly;
Though I am but clay and dust,
Yet thy grace can lift me high.
—THOMAS CAMPION (English, 1567–1620)

SCRIPTURES

PSALM 90 | JOEL 2:12–17 | REVELATION 18:9–19 | LUKE 18:9–14

READINGS

From "In Memoriam A.H.H." by ALFRED, LORD TENNYSON
"Ash Wednesday" by ANYA SILVER
"Blood in the Snow" by GREGORY SPENCER
"Jung's Shadow and Matthew 4:16" by MARCI RAE JOHNSON
"1 Corinthians 13:11" by JERICHO BROWN
"The Litany" by DANA GIOIA
From "The Minister's Black Veil: A Parable" by NATHANIEL HAWTHORNE

PERSONAL PRAYER AND REFLECTION

CLOSING PRAYER

Our eyes shall see thee, which before saw dust;
     Dust blown by wit, till that they both were blind:
     Thou shalt recover all thy goods in kind,
Who wert diseased by usurping lust:

All knees shall bow to thee; all wits shall rise,
And praise him who did make and mend our eyes.
— GEORGE HERBERT (English, 1593–1633)

#### READINGS

FROM *"In Memoriam A.H.H."*
ALFRED, LORD TENNYSON (English, 1809–1892)

Strong Son of God, immortal Love,
　Whom we, that have not seen thy face,
　By faith, and faith alone, embrace,
Believing where we cannot prove;

Thine are these orbs of light and shade;
　Thou madest Life in man and brute;
　Thou madest Death; and lo, thy foot
Is on the skull which thou hast made.

Thou wilt not leave us in the dust:
　Thou madest man, he knows not why;
　He thinks he was not made to die;
And thou hast made him: thou art just.

Thou seemest human and divine,
　The highest, holiest manhood, thou:
　Our wills are ours, we know not how;
Our wills are ours, to make them thine.

Our little systems have their day;
　They have their day and cease to be:
　They are but broken lights of thee,
And thou, O Lord, art more than they.

We have but faith: we cannot know;
   For knowledge is of things we see;
   And yet we trust it comes from thee,
A beam in darkness: let it grow.

Let knowledge grow from more to more,
   But more of reverence in us dwell;
   That mind and soul, according well,
May make one music as before,

But vaster. We are fools and slight;
   We mock thee when we do not fear:
   But help thy foolish ones to bear;
Help thy vain worlds to bear thy light.

––––––

## *Ash Wednesday*

ANYA SILVER (Anglo-American, contemporary)

How comforting, the smudge on each forehead:
I'm not to be singled out after all
*From dust you came. To dust you will return.*
My mastectomy, a *memento mori*,[2]
prosthesis smooth as a polished skull.
I like the solidarity of this prayer,
the ointment thumbed into my forehead,
my knees pressing hard on the velvet rail.
If God won't give me His body to clutch,
I'll grind this soot into my skin instead.
If I can't hold the flame that burned my breast,
I'll char my brow; I'll blacken my pores; I'll flaunt
with ash this flaw in His creation.

––––––

## Blood in the Snow
GREGORY SPENCER (Anglo-American, contemporary)

I have yet to see a crimson cardinal,
though Virginia boasts he's there waiting
      on some blossomed branch whistling.

Perhaps a blood-red bird will soon appear
against this winter-white ash
      that floats down graceful from God's chimney.

Our children have fallen—we all have—
and bear hot bruises from these icy slips.
      Undeterred, they surf the slopes this March,

calculating pace and angles for success.
I sent them out today in striped shirts
      to crunch and slide near the Holocaust museum.

Just yesterday a man was murdered there. I remember
the news said he did nothing wrong;
      but I let the children go anyway,

to walk that path where winter's
white ash falls from God's chimney
      and I've yet to see a cardinal.

———

## Jung's Shadow and Matthew 4:16
MARCI RAE JOHNSON (Anglo-American, contemporary)

Even in winter there was sun living
in the green shoulders of the waves.
I'd walk the beach alone with shadows:
gulls in formation on the ground.
Once the bones. Once a poem

that wrote itself behind my eyes.
When I'd come home he wouldn't say
how much he feared the way I'd carry
words to the clouds and let them go.
*Everyone carries a shadow.* Everyone

breathes out fog in the cold. Even
the living sun can't melt the ice shelf
that pushes up the sand, makes
of this familiar scape a wild shape –
a place that can't be known.

I walk the dunes above, misplace
the old theologies. I suppose a light
has dawned. The sun pushed high
as it will get, tapping the tops of pines,

my own shadow long among
the others growing darker, denser
the more I call the light
to me. The more I try to see.

———

## 1 *Corinthians* 13:11

JERICHO BROWN (African-American, contemporary)

When I was a child, I spoke as a child.
I even had a child's disease. I ran
From the Doberman like all children
On my street, but old men called me
Special. The Doberman caught up,
Chewed my right knee. Limp now
In two places, I carried a child's Bible
Like a football under the arm that didn't

Ache. I was never alone. I owned
My brother's shame of me. I loved
The words *thou* and *thee*. Both meant
My tongue in front of my teeth.
Both meant a someone speaking to me.
So what if I itched. So what if I couldn't
Breathe. I climbed the cyclone fence
Like children on my street and went
First when old men asked for a boy
To pray or to read. Some had it worse—
Nobody whipped me with a water hose
Or a phone cord or a leash. Old men
Said I'd grow into my face, and I did.

———

## The Litany

DANA GIOIA (Anglo-American, contemporary)

This is a litany of lost things,
a canon of possessions dispossessed,
a photograph, an old address, a key.
It is a list of words to memorize
or to forget—of *amo, amas, amat*,[3]
the conjugations of a dead tongue
in which the final sentence has been spoken.

This is the liturgy of rain,
falling on mountain, field, and ocean—
indifferent, anonymous, complete—
of water infinitesimally slow,
sifting through rock, pooling in darkness,
gathering in springs, then rising without our agency,
only to dissolve in mist or cloud or dew.

This is a prayer to unbelief,
to candles guttering and darkness undivided,
to incense drifting into emptiness.
It is the smile of a stone Madonna
and the silent fury of the consecrated wine,
a benediction on the death of a young god,
brave and beautiful, rotting on a tree.

This is a litany to earth and ashes,
to the dust of roads and vacant rooms,
to the fine silt circling in a shaft of sun,
settling indifferently on books and beds.
This is a prayer to praise what we become,
"Dust thou art, to dust thou shalt return."
Savor its taste—the bitterness of earth and ashes.

This is a prayer, inchoate and unfinished,
for you, my love, my loss, my lesion,
a rosary of words to count out time's
illusions, all the minutes, hours days
the calendar compounds as if the past
existed somewhere—like an inheritance
still waiting to be claimed.

Until at last it is our litany, *mon vieux*,[4]
my reader, my voyeur, as if the mist
steaming from the gorge, this pure paradox,
the shattered river rising as it falls—
splintering the light, swirling it skyward,
neither transparent nor opaque but luminous,
even as it vanishes—were not our life.

———

FROM *"The Minister's Black Veil: A Parable"*
NATHANIEL HAWTHORNE (Anglo-American, 1804–1864)

The sexton stood in the porch of Milford meeting-house pulling lustily at the bell-rope. The old people of the village came stooping along the street. Children with bright faces tripped merrily beside their parents or mimicked a graver gait in the conscious dignity of their Sunday clothes. Spruce bachelors looked sidelong at the pretty maidens, and fancied that the Sabbath sunshine made them prettier than on week-days. When the throng had mostly streamed into the porch, the sexton began to toll the bell, keeping his eye on the Reverend Mr. Hooper's door. The first glimpse of the clergyman's figure was the signal for the bell to cease its summons.

"But what has good Parson Hooper got upon his face?" cried the sexton, in astonishment.

All within hearing immediately turned about and beheld the semblance of Mr. Hooper pacing slowly his meditative way toward the meeting-house. With one accord they started, expressing more wonder than if some strange minister were coming to dust the cushions of Mr. Hooper's pulpit.

"Are you sure it is our parson?" inquired Goodman Gray of the sexton.

"Of a certainty it is good Mr. Hooper," replied the sexton. "He was to have exchanged pulpits with Parson Shute of Westbury, but Parson Shute sent to excuse himself yesterday, being to preach a funeral sermon."

The cause of so much amazement may appear sufficiently slight. Mr. Hooper, a gentlemanly person of about thirty, though still a bachelor, was dressed with due clerical neatness, as if a careful wife had starched his band and brushed the weekly dust from his Sunday's garb. There was but one thing remarkable in his appearance. Swathed about his forehead and hanging down over his face, so low as to be shaken by his breath, Mr. Hooper had on a black veil. On a nearer view it seemed to consist of two folds of crape, which entirely concealed his features except the mouth and chin, but probably did not intercept his sight further than to give a darkened aspect to all living and inanimate things. With this gloomy shade before him good Mr. Hooper walked onward at a slow and quiet pace, stooping somewhat and looking on the ground, as is customary with abstracted men, yet nodding kindly to those of his parishioners who still waited on the meeting-house steps. But so wonder-struck were they that his greeting hardly met with a return.

"I can't really feel as if good Mr. Hooper's face was behind that piece of crape," said the sexton.

"I don't like it," muttered an old woman as she hobbled into the meeting-house. "He has changed himself into something awful only by hiding his face."

"Our parson has gone mad!" cried Goodman Gray, following him across the threshold.

A rumor of some unaccountable phenomenon had preceded Mr. Hooper into the meeting-house and set all the congregation astir. Few could refrain from twisting their heads toward the door; many stood upright and turned directly about; while several little boys clambered upon the seats, and came down again with a terrible racket. There was a general bustle, a rustling of the women's gowns and shuffling of the men's feet, greatly at variance with that hushed repose which should attend the entrance of the minister. But Mr. Hooper appeared not to notice the perturbation of his people. He entered with an almost noiseless step, bent his head mildly to the pews on each side and bowed as he passed his oldest parishioner, a white-haired great-grandsire, who occupied an arm-chair in the center of the aisle. It was strange to observe how slowly this venerable man became conscious of something singular in the appearance of his pastor. He seemed not fully to partake of the prevailing wonder till Mr. Hooper had ascended the stairs and showed himself in the pulpit, face to face with his congregation except for the black veil.

That mysterious emblem was never once withdrawn. It shook with his measured breath as he gave out the psalm, it threw its obscurity between him and the holy page as he read the Scriptures, and while he prayed the veil lay heavily on his uplifted countenance. Did he seek to hide it from the dread Being whom he was addressing?

Such was the effect of this simple piece of crape that more than one woman of delicate nerves was forced to leave the meeting-house. Yet perhaps the pale-faced congregation was almost as fearful a sight to the minister as his black veil to them.

Mr. Hooper had the reputation of a good preacher, but not an energetic one: he strove to win his people heavenward by mild, persuasive influences rather than to drive them thither by the thunders of the word. The sermon which he now delivered was marked by the same characteristics of style and manner as the general series of his pulpit oratory, but there was something either in the sentiment of the discourse itself or in the imagination of the auditors which made it greatly the most powerful effort that they had ever heard from their pastor's lips. It was tinged rather more darkly than usual with the gentle gloom of Mr. Hooper's temperament. The subject had reference to secret sin and those sad mysteries which we hide from our nearest and dearest, and would fain conceal from our own consciousness, even forgetting that the Omniscient can detect them. A subtle power was breathed into his words. Each member of the congregation, the most innocent girl and the man of hardened breast, felt as if the preacher had crept upon them behind his awful veil and discovered their hoarded iniquity of deed or thought. Many spread their clasped hands on their bosoms. There was nothing terrible in what Mr. Hooper said—at least, no violence; and yet with every tremor of his melancholy voice the hearers quaked. An unsought pathos came hand in hand with awe. So sensible were the audience of some unwonted attribute in their minister that they longed for a breath of wind to blow aside the veil, almost believing that a stranger's visage would be discovered, though the form, gesture and voice were those of Mr. Hooper.

At the close of the services the people hurried out with indecorous confusion, eager to communicate their pent-up amazement, and conscious of lighter spirits the moment they lost sight of the black veil. Some gathered in little circles, huddled closely together, with their mouths all whispering in the center; some went homeward alone, wrapped in silent meditation; some talked loudly and profaned the Sabbath-day with ostentatious laughter. A few shook their sagacious heads, intimating that they could penetrate the mystery, while one or two affirmed that there was no mystery at all, but only that Mr. Hooper's eyes were so weakened by the midnight lamp as to require a shade.

After a brief interval forth came good Mr. Hooper also, in the rear of his flock. Turning his veiled face from one group to another, he paid due reverence to the hoary heads, saluted the middle-aged with kind dignity as their friend and spiritual guide, greeted the young with mingled authority and love, and laid his hands on the little children's heads to bless them. Such was always his custom on the Sabbath-day. Strange and bewildered looks repaid him for his courtesy. None, as on former occasions, aspired to the honor of walking by their pastor's side. Old Squire Saunders—doubtless by an accidental lapse of memory—neglected to invite Mr. Hooper to his table, where the good clergyman had been wont to bless the food almost every Sunday since his settlement. He returned, therefore, to the parsonage, and at the moment of closing the door was observed to look back upon the people, all of whom had their eyes fixed upon the minister. A sad smile gleamed faintly from beneath the black veil and flickered about his mouth, glimmering as he disappeared.

"How strange," said a lady, "that a simple black veil, such as any woman might wear on her bonnet, should become such a terrible thing on Mr. Hooper's face!"

"Something must surely be amiss with Mr. Hooper's intellects," observed her husband, the physician of the village. "But the strangest part of the affair is the effect of this vagary even on a sober-minded man like myself. The black veil, though it covers only our pastor's face, throws its influence over his whole person and makes him ghost-like from head to foot. Do you not feel it so?"

"Truly do I," replied the lady; "and I would not be alone with him for the world. I wonder he is not afraid to be alone with himself."

"Men sometimes are so," said her husband. . . .

## LENT WEEK 1

## *The Way of Negation*

### OPENING PRAYER

Lord, wave again the chastening rod,
Till every idol throne
Crumble to dust, and thou, O God,
Reign in our hearts alone.
—JOHN KEBLE (English, 1792–1866)

### SCRIPTURES

PSALM 42 | ISAIAH 58:1–5 | 2 CORINTHIANS 6:1–10 | MATTHEW 16:21–28

### READINGS

"Letter To Saint Francis" by ABIGAIL CARROLL
"To Keep a True Lent" by ROBERT HERRICK
"New Mexico, 1992" by BENJAMÍN ALIRE SÁENZ
"Later Life: A Double Sonnet of Sonnets (II)" by CHRISTINA ROSSETTI
"Seventeens: Acoustics" by AMIT MAJMUDAR
From *Brendan* by FREDERICK BUECHNER

### PERSONAL PRAYER AND REFLECTION

### CLOSING PRAYER

look o lord
i don't sing your praises
but i seek you
with my limbs
which i've tamed just for you
for i want to keep watch over your word

so that love be found anew
and we win back our wildness.
—SAID (Iranian, contemporary)


### READINGS


## Letter To Saint Francis
ABIGAIL CARROLL (Anglo-American, contemporary)

When you broke with the world, you gave up jerkins and boots
    (Italian leather, no less),

the title to your name. In light of your example, I hereby forsake
    (not wanting to duplicate)

the paisley, polarized shades I have wanted to buy for some months
    (now on sale at Rite Aid),

plans for a new voile spread and matching shams—you see, my room
    (unaltered in years),

is begging for a complete re-do. In addition, I forthwith happily resign
    (and with only a little shame)

my ignorance of bird songs, apathy toward insects, and above all else
    (no simple task)

my solemn right to complain—about weather, fractures, vacuuming,
    (the Lord gives)

or the sudden need for new axels, a change of plans, someone to love
    (the Lord takes away).

I'd also like to swear off phones, hornets, gas stations, the news,
    (and, while I'm at it)

the banality of prose. When it comes to relinquishing clothes, I can
    (most definitely)

do without nylons and heels, and that black bridesmaid shawl I prized
    (but never wore),

which has hung in my closet for years. Abandoning these worldly goods
    (I sincerely trust)

will also mean the giving up of dust in all its forms: dandruff, worry,
shame,
    (bathtub residues)—

In truth, Francis, there are many things I'd like to lose.

———

## To Keep a True Lent
ROBERT HERRICK (English, 1591–1674)

Is this a fast, to keep
    The larder lean?
        And clean
From fat of veals and sheep?

Is it to quit the dish
    Of flesh, yet still
        To fill
The platter high with fish?

Is it to fast an hour,
    Or ragg'd to go,
        Or show
A downcast look and sour?

No; 'tis a fast to dole
    Thy sheaf of wheat,
        And meat,
Unto the hungry soul.

It is to fast from strife,
   From old debate
      And hate;
To circumcise thy life.

To show a heart grief-rent;
   To starve thy sin,
      Not bin;
And that's to keep thy Lent.

———

## New Mexico, 1992
BENJAMÍN ALIRE SÁENZ (Mexican-American, contemporary)

We learned to make the sign
                     of the cross,
Dipping earth stained hands in Catholic

Waters. We've filled the desert
                     with our altars.
We prayed our rosaries, played them,

Rubbed them, clutched them—
                     rattles in the wind
Swaying back and forth—our

Playground swings, we rode them
                     toward God,
Now hang them on walls or rear view

Mirrors of fixed-up '57 trucks.
                     Comenzamos
el Padre Nuestro en español[5] but we

finish the prayer in a North

                American tongue.

De vez en cuando[6] we gather

ourselves together to baptize

                a child

in the name of the Father, the Son,

and our ancestors who command us

                from the grave.

We have made our way in the world,

worked hard, worked hard. Now, we

                toss money

at the feet of my parent's grandchildren

like pilgrims tossed palms

                before Christ.

In the sounds of our coins against

the concrete, I hear novenas

                yellowing into dust.

We try to speak of our lives

purely. Our memories will not

                let us.

We wear our culture as penitents

wear ashes on their foreheads,

                Una mancha

Permanente.[7] We wake in strange-streeted

cities with the taste of the desert
                              in our mouths.
Because we are hungry, the taste

is sweet. We are damned to live
                              forever
on a border. From here, we build

our altars to our gods.

――――

## Later Life: A Double Sonnet of Sonnets (II)
CHRISTINA ROSSETTI (English, 1830–1894)

Rend hearts and rend not garments for our sins;
   Gird sackcloth not on body but on soul;
   Grovel in dust with faces toward the goal
Nor won, nor neared: he only laughs who wins.
Not neared the goal, the race too late begins;
   Or left undone, we have yet to do the whole;
   The sun is hurrying west and toward the pole
Where darkness waits for earth with all her kins.
Let us to-day, while it is called to-day,
   Set out, if utmost speed may yet avail—
   The shadows lengthen and the light grows pale:
     For who through darkness and the shadow of death,
Darkness that may be felt, shall find a way,
   Blind-eyed, deaf-eared, and choked with failing breath?

――――

## Seventeens: Acoustics

AMIT MAJMUDAR (Indian-American, contemporary)

A hand must pass the strings for them to sound.
The absence of the touch is what resounds.
Axon for axon, we are strung, we are
A kind of neurological guitar
A star has strummed to music. Our musician
Has touched us once, gone quiet now to listen—
Is this mind flat or sharp? How well's it tuned?
The absence of his hand is opportune,
His famous silence proof we have his ear.
Reverberation needs the aisles clear,
And rumination needs some room to roam.
If he were here, these rhymes would stay at home,
And all that's hard and hardest-won in us
Be obviated by the obvious.
Have your hosannah, I prefer the hush.
Check the acoustics in this empty hall.
Not the faintest echo when you call.

———

## FROM *Brendan*

FREDERICK BUECHNER (Anglo-American, contemporary)

[Editor's note: Sixth-century Ireland comes alive in all its mess and mystery with this rich, humorous, poignant portrait of Saint Brendan the Navigator as told by his good friend and follower, Finn. Here, the young teenage Brendan—who is growing up among a monastic community led by Abbot Jarlath—has fled to a cave to seek God's mercy for being in danger of lust.]

A scrawny hollow-chested wreck of a boy he was at the time, half wore out with growing too fast and dragging his dirty big feet about with him wherever he went. The sky outside was black as death and the cave blacker yet. Jarlath said he wasn't in a state of mortal sin but Jarlath didn't know all of it. He didn't know how in his heart the boy wallowed in sinfulness like a sow in muck, how he thirsted for it like the mixed wine in the navel of the Shulamite woman King Solomon sung of in his holy song or the honey and milk the song said was under her tongue.

Brendan's teeth was chattering so hard his words come out all stuttery like a half-wit's gobble. He prayed as many prayers as he knew of and said as many psalms as he'd ever learned. He stirred in as many Laus-laus-laus tibis and De Profun-fun-fundises and Pater no-no-nosters as he had breath for. There was such a fearsome buzzing in his ears he was afraid it might be the gentry[8] coming for him with their tongues in their cheeks and pulling their eyes into slits with their thumbs. It wasn't like praying for some special thing like his enemies' herds to get blacktongue or the sore on Briga's lip to heal because there wasn't some one simple thing like that he wanted just then. The one thing he knew he ought to want was what he didn't want at all. It was the quenching of the fires of sin inside him. Only he didn't want them quenched. Instead he hungered for them all the more.

No matter how high the boy aimed his holy gobbling skyward though he didn't reach an ear to hear him far as he could tell anyhow. There wasn't so much as a whisker of starlight or moonlight in the sky or anything else you might have cared to call a sign of the mercy of God or anything else of God. There was only emptiness and darkness like God had gone off altogether carrying his mercy with him on his shoulder like the Dagda[9] carrying his six-string harp.

Nobody ever tried harder at making God hear surely. He called on him till the veins on his neck swelled and his face went black. He kept at it till one eye got sucked deep into the socket and the other bulged out like a berry on a stem. He gaped his jaws at Heaven till his lips peeled back from his teeth and you could see down to where his lungs and liver was flapping like fish in a basket. Up out of the point of his head a jet of his heart's blood spurted black and smoking. That's how he told it.

"There came angels at last, Finn," he said. "They were spread out against the sky like a great wreath. The closest were close enough to touch nearly. The farthest were farther than the stars. I never saw so many stars. I could hear the stillness of them they were that still."

I see his pinched face go silvery watching. There's silver in the hollows of his cheeks. He has silver eyes. His shoulderblades cast shadows dark as wings on his bony boy's back.

"Lofty and fair beyond telling was the angels' music," he said. "They heard me cry and they answered me. They weren't singing to me of the mercy of God, Finn. Their singing was itself the mercy of God. Do you think I could ever forget it even if I tried?"

Two things followed from that night in the cave.

One of them was he shunned the company of women from that time forth.

The other was that ever afterwards he wore a string about his neck with a ball of beeswax at each of its two ends. Whenever there was music or singing of any kind at all he'd work the balls into his ears saying he wanted nothing on this earth to make him ever forget the music of Heaven next to which the sweetest trill of birds even was like the yammering of cats and made his head ache like somebody was pounding on it with a stone.

## LENT WEEK 2

## *The Place of Desolation*

### OPENING PRAYER

Welcome, my grief, my joy; how dear's
To me my legacy of tears!
I'll weep and weep, and will therefore
Weep 'cause I can weep no more.
Thou, thou, dear Lord, even thou alone,
Giv'st joy, even when thou givest none.
—RICHARD CRASHAW (English, 1612–1649)

### SCRIPTURES

PSALM 13 | ISAIAH 6:1–5 | 1 JOHN 3:18–24 | LUKE 13:22–30

### READINGS

"The Road to Damascus: 6" by TANIA RUNYAN
"we lifted our eyes to the hills" by JOHN FRY
"Thou hast made me (Divine Meditations: I)" by JOHN DONNE
"I have stood at the center of the world" by CATHERINE MCNIEL
"My prayers must meet a brazen heaven" by GERARD MANLEY HOPKINS
"An Apprehension" by ELIZABETH BARRETT BROWNING

### PERSONAL PRAYER AND REFLECTION

### CLOSING PRAYER

If I have played the truant, or have here
Failed in my part, oh! Thou that art my dear,
My mild, my loving tutor, Lord and God!
Correct my errors gently with thy rod.

I know that faults will many here be found,
But where sin swells there let thy grace abound.
— ROBERT HERRICK (English, 1591-1674)

### READINGS

## The Road to Damascus: 6
TANIA RUNYAN (Anglo-American, Contemporary)

I have sinned, I said.
I want eternal life, I said.
That was the moment.
I wanted nothing but God.
I wanted a cheeseburger.
I wanted nothing at all.
Finally, I wanted it all settled.
I folded my hands and spoke
to the carpet. I folded my hands
and spoke to the Lord.
I woke up and felt no different.
I woke up and my life
came to an end.

———

## we lifted our eyes to the hills
JOHN FRY (Anglo-American, contemporary)

how we'd lifted burnt
offerings, our hearts. as shorn

        things bleat, cling. for help
        had not come. for our

bramble-bloodied feet
slipped—He slept—
        shadowed by absence of
        outstretched, His hand could

stave neither solar nor
oxidized green flares
        of moonglare watching over us,
        insomniac. we knew not

why the slow subtraction (devil's
arithmetic) of our right wrist
        bones clamored, cold. pursued
        not by what, but whom were

heavy-laden we looking, for
Lord—where smoke risen from
        a ram's scapula was its lampblack
        psalm. to the hills we lifted

our eyes, threadbare antiphons,
deserts away from where we were
        promised benediction, our goodbyes
        blackened, our altars. help had not come.

———

## 'Thou hast made me' (Divine Meditations: I)
JOHN DONNE (English, 1572–1631)

Thou hast made me, and shall thy work decay?
Repair me now, for now mine end doth haste,
I run to death, and death meets me as fast,

And all my pleasures are like yesterday;
I dare not move my dim eyes any way,
Despair behind, and death before doth cast
Such terror, and my feeble flesh doth waste
By sin in it, which it towards hell doth weigh;
Only thou art above, and when towards thee
By thy leave I can look, I rise again;
But our old subtle foe so tempteth me,
That not one hour myself I can sustain;
Thy Grace may wing me to prevent his art,
And thou like adamant draw mine iron heart.

———

## 'I have stood at the center of the world'
CATHERINE McNIEL (Anglo-American, contemporary)

I have stood at the center of the world
The primordial Tree, the innocent Beginning
I have been rejected there, exiled
So I wander
Homeless, yet seeking Home
Marked, yet seeking

I have traveled so far in my wanderings
That I have changed, the distance became a chasm
And yet I have stayed so closely tied
Lingering near with hope for Healing
Longing

I stand in the place of Anger and Accusation
Watching the last box of bitterness carried out the door
Alone now with the vast emptiness in its place
There's nothing left to do but this endless
Wandering and lingering

I have forgiven
But you have forgotten
Even a child casts her own shadow
The past has built itself into my body and soul
And there it is:
The bruised and fallen apple is its own seed

———

## 'My prayers must meet a brazen heaven'
GERARD MANLEY HOPKINS (English, 1844–1889)

My prayers must meet a brazen heaven
And fail and scatter all away.
Unclean and seeming unforgiven
My prayers I scarcely call to pray.
I cannot buoy my heart above;
Above I cannot entrance win.
I reckon precedents of love,
But feel the long success of sin.

My heaven is brass and iron my earth:
Yea, iron is mingled with my clay,
So harden'd is it in this dearth
Which praying fails to do away.
Nor tears, nor tears this clay uncouth
Could mould, if any tears there were.
A warfare of my lips in truth,
Battling with God, is now my prayer.

———

## An Apprehension

ELIZABETH BARRETT BROWNING (English, 1806–1861)

If all the gentlest-hearted friends I know
Concentrated in one heart their gentleness,
That still grew gentler till its pulse was less
For life than pity,—I should yet be slow
To bring my own heart nakedly below
The palm of such a friend, that he should press
Motive, condition, means, appliances,
My false ideal joy and fickle woe,
Out full to light and knowledge; I should fear
Some plait between the brows, some rougher chime
In the free voice. O angels, let your flood
Of bitter scorn dash on me! do ye hear
What *I* say who bear calmly all the time
This everlasting face to face with God?

———

## FROM *Emma*

JANE AUSTEN (English, 1775–1817)

[Editor's note: Two hundred years have passed, and yet Jane Austen's ability to probe the complex psychology of self-deception makes her one of the greatest novelists of all time. In Emma, we are given a bright, wealthy, generally good-hearted young woman who has developed the bad habit of manipulating relationships at others' expense. It's a trend of which her good friend and brother-in-law, Mr. Knightley, does not approve. So when, on a group picnic, Emma makes a public jab at another old family friend—the poor, unmarried, talkative Miss Bates—Mr. Knightley speaks his mind. His honest words become a mirror Emma doesn't wish to look into but must.]

While waiting for the carriage, she found Mr. Knightley by her side. He looked around, as if to see that no one were near, and then said,

"Emma, I must once more speak to you as I have been used to do: a privilege rather endured than allowed, perhaps, but I must still use it. I cannot see you acting wrong, without a remonstrance. How could you be so unfeeling to Miss Bates? How could you be so insolent in your wit to a woman of her character, age, and situation?—Emma, I had not thought it possible."

Emma recollected, blushed, was sorry, but tried to laugh it off.

"Nay, how could I help saying what I did?—Nobody could have helped it. It was not so very bad. I dare say she did not understand me."

"I assure you she did. She felt your full meaning. She has talked of it since. I wish you could have heard how she talked of it— with what candor and generosity. I wish you could have heard her honoring your forbearance, in being able to pay her such attentions, as she was for ever receiving from yourself and your father, when her society must be so irksome."

"Oh!" cried Emma, "I know there is not a better creature in the world: but you must allow, that what is good and what is ridiculous are most unfortunately blended in her."

"They are blended," said he, "I acknowledge; and, were she prosperous, I could allow much for the occasional prevalence of the ridiculous over the good. Were she a woman of fortune, I would leave every harmless absurdity to take its chance, I would not quarrel with you for any liberties of manner. Were she your equal in situation—but, Emma, consider how far this is from being the case. She is poor; she has sunk from the comforts she was born to; and, if she live to old age, must probably sink more. Her situation should secure your compassion. It was badly done, indeed! You, whom she had known from an infant, whom she had seen grow up from a period when her notice was an honor, to have you now, in thoughtless spirits, and the pride of the moment, laugh at her, humble her—and before her niece, too—and before others, many of whom (certainly *some*,) would be entirely guided by *your* treatment of her.—This is not pleasant to you, Emma—and it is very far from pleasant to me; but I must, I will,—I will tell you truths while I can; satisfied with proving myself your friend by very faithful counsel, and trusting that you will some time or other do me greater justice than you can do now."

While they talked, they were advancing towards the carriage; it was ready; and, before she could speak again, he had handed her in. He had misinterpreted the feelings which had kept her face averted, and her tongue motionless. They were combined only of anger against herself, mortification, and deep concern. She had not been able to speak; and, on entering the carriage, sunk back for a moment overcome— then reproaching herself for having taken no leave, making no acknowledgment, parting in apparent sullenness, she looked out with voice and hand eager to show a difference; but it was just too late. He had turned away, and the horses were in motion. She continued to look back, but in vain; and soon, with what appeared unusual speed, they were half way down the hill, and every thing left far behind. She was vexed beyond what could have been expressed—almost beyond what she could conceal. Never had she felt so agitated, mortified, grieved, at any circumstance in her life. She was most forcibly struck. The truth of this representation there was no denying. She felt it at her heart. How could she have been so brutal, so cruel to Miss Bates! How could she have exposed herself to such ill opinion in any one she valued! And how suffer him to leave her without saying one word of gratitude, of concurrence, of common kindness!

Time did not compose her. As she reflected more, she seemed but to feel it more. She never had been so depressed. Happily it was not necessary to speak. There was only Harriet, who seemed not in spirits herself, fagged, and very willing to be silent; and Emma felt the tears running down her cheeks almost all the way home, without being at any trouble to check them, extraordinary as they were.

# LENT WEEK 3

## *Secret Terrors*

OPENING PRAYER
lord
a great sorrow has come upon me
the word has overpowered me
so teach me to keep still
so that i might begin to love you
and have mercy upon me
for my dwelling is built of memory
i fear the straight line of logic
and lose myself in the body's mystery
—SAID (Iranian, contemporary)

SCRIPTURES
PSALM 38 | LAMENTATIONS 3:1–20 | ROMANS 7:14–25 | LUKE 7:1–10

READINGS
"The Faith of the Roman Centurion" by MARCI RAE JOHNSON
"My own heart" by GERARD MANLEY HOPKINS
"Catechism" by BRETT FOSTER
"Evening Prayer" by SCOTT CAIRNS
"Like His, Confessions" by GREGORY SPENCER
From *The Secret Garden* by FRANCES HODGSON BURNETT

PERSONAL PRAYER AND REFLECTION

CLOSING PRAYER

Please, may the horrible abyss not separate
me from those you have redeemed.
Please, may the corrupt, corrupting enemy
not hinder my path to You.
Please, if by any human weakness
I have sinned in word or deed or thought,
may my sin pass unnoticed by Your sight.
—MACRINA THE YOUNGER (Turkish, ca. 327–379)
adapted by Scott Cairns

# READINGS

## *The Faith of the Roman Centurion*
MARCI RAE JOHNSON (Anglo-American, contemporary)

Today Jesus has performed 12,100,000 miracles
on Google. In .38 seconds, he has stretched out
his hand and healed at a distance the servant,
the little girl, the mother-in-law. He has warmed
my hand on the television set, through the man
who has promised healing if I confess.
Though I am paralyzed, I kneel on the hard
wood, palms against the grain, the bone-colored
sponge, making everything clean for the one
who takes possession next: my home, my heart.
Though you rolled me over in the morning
when I couldn't move, though you held my ribs
between your hands and drew my breath, still
you have gone and not returned. The phone
lies prostrate on the floor, my back against the wall,

arms not willing to lift themselves. It is a state
of being. *Helpless stoppage, inability to act.*
Have you gone to find help? To tell the Lord
I am lying at home, fearfully tormented?

––––

## 'My own heart'
GERARD MANLEY HOPKINS (English, 1844–1889)

My own heart let me more have pity on; let
Me live to my sad self hereafter kind,
Charitable; not live this tormented mind
With this tormented mind tormenting yet.

I cast for comfort I can no more get
By groping round my comfortless than blind
Eyes in their dark can day or thirst can find
Thirst's all-in-all in all a world of wet.

Soul, self; come, poor Jackself, I do advise
You, jaded, let be; call off thoughts awhile
Elsewhere; leave comfort root-room; let joy size

At God knows when to God knows what; whose smile
's not wrung, see you; unforeseentimes rather—as skies
Betweenpie mountains—lights a lovely mile.

––––

## Catechism
BRETT FOSTER (Anglo-American, contemporary)

*What sort of belief would you say is yours?*
Porous. Calibrated to the times. The week.

*In what ways has superflux affected you?*
Too much esteem. Tuned finely to the body's work.

*What do you fear has not been delivered?*
The disease of courage. Will it be required?

*No questions, please. Can you see yourself tested?*
I have never suffered for anything.

*In how many dimensions is your faith?*
One thin one, at least. [Aside] Was that a trick question?

*What is the single thing that sustains you?*
Abiding hope that being here's made good.

*Care to clarify? Care to offer last words?*
I offer essentially nothing, but enough—

———

## Evening Prayer

Scott Cairns (Anglo-American, contemporary)

And what *would* you pray in the troubled midst
of this our circular confusion save
that the cup be taken away? That the chill
and welling of the blood might suffer by His
hushed mercy to abate, to calm the legion
dumb anxieties as each now clamors
to be known and named? The road has taken
on, of late, the mute appearance of a grief
whose leaden gravity both insists on speed
and slows the pilgrim's progress to a crawl.
At least he's found his knees. I bear a dim
suspicion that this circumstance will hold
unyielding hegemony until the day.

What *would* you pray at the approach of this
late evening? What ask? And of whom?

———

## Like His, Confessions
GREGORY SPENCER (Anglo-American, contemporary)

When I'm feeling well after
these years of pain,

magnanimity reigns. I know
why I have suffered

thus and I rise
to teach about the struggle.

Like Augustine, I see God
at my back, pushing me from aching rib

to unlocked hip, from the Carthage of
my tender cartilage to the Rome

of good bones. Oh how much I've changed
—I think—then the torment returns,

spilling over the brim of the Bishop's cup
and I find I'm drowning

all over again. Swept out, sucked
in, flooded, I sink fast, and my fingers go up.

And down. Four. Three. Two. One.
Grab me now.

———

FROM *The Secret Garden*

FRANCES HODGSON BURNETT (English-American, 1849–1924)

[Editor's note: Orphaned Mary Lennox—spoiled, sickly, petulant—has left the only life she's ever known in India to become the ward of her mostly absent, hunchback uncle in a grim manor on a lonely moor in England. Soon she discovers a secret: her uncle has a son, about her age, named Colin, hidden away in a wing of the house. Everyone treats Colin as an invalid who will become a hunchback like his father, and Colin in turn has become selfish and demanding. He and Mary strike up an unlikely friendship that leads to the following confrontation.]

She thought it was the middle of the night when she was wakened by such dreadful sounds that she jumped out of bed in an instant. What was it—what was it? The next minute she felt quite sure she knew. Doors were opened and shut and there were hurrying feet in the corridors and some one was crying and screaming at the same time, screaming and crying in a horrible way.

"It's Colin," she said. "He's having one of those tantrums the nurse called hysterics. How awful it sounds."

As she listened to the sobbing screams she did not wonder that people were so frightened that they gave him his own way in everything rather than hear them. She put her hands over her ears and felt sick and shivering.

"I don't know what to do. I don't know what to do," she kept saying. "I can't bear it."

Once she wondered if he would stop if she dared go to him and then she remembered how he had driven her out of the room and thought that perhaps the sight of her might make him worse. Even when she pressed her hands more tightly over her ears she could not keep the awful sounds out. She hated them so and was so terrified by them that suddenly they began to make her angry and she felt as if she should like to fly into a tantrum herself and frighten him as he was frightening her. She was not used to any one's tempers but her own. She took her hands from her ears and sprang up and stamped her foot.

"He ought to be stopped! Somebody ought to make him stop! Somebody ought to beat him!" she cried out.

Just then she heard feet almost running down the corridor and her door opened and the nurse came in. She was not laughing now by any means. She even looked rather pale.

"He's worked himself into hysterics," she said in a great hurry. "He'll do himself harm. No one can do anything with him. You come and try, like a good child. He likes you."

"He turned me out of the room this morning," said Mary, stamping her foot with excitement.

The stamp rather pleased the nurse. The truth was that she had been afraid she might find Mary crying and hiding her head under the bed-clothes.

"That's right," she said. "You're in the right humor. You go and scold him. Give him something new to think of. Do go, child, as quick as ever you can."

It was not until afterward that Mary realized that the thing had been funny as well as dreadful—that it was funny that all the grown-up people were so frightened that they came to a little girl just because they guessed she was almost as bad as Colin himself.

She flew along the corridor and the nearer she got to the screams the higher her temper mounted. She felt quite wicked by the time she reached the door. She slapped it open with her hand and ran across the room to the four-posted bed.

"You stop!" she almost shouted. "You stop! I hate you! Everybody hates you! I wish everybody would run out of the house and let you scream yourself to death! You *will* scream yourself to death in a minute, and I wish you would!"

A nice sympathetic child could neither have thought nor said such things, but it just happened that the shock of hearing them was the best possible thing for this hysterical boy whom no one had ever dared to restrain or contradict.

He had been lying on his face beating his pillow with his hands and he actually almost jumped around, he turned so quickly at the sound of the furious little voice. His face looked dreadful, white and red and swollen, and he was gasping and choking; but savage little Mary did not care an atom.

"If you scream another scream," she said, "I'll scream too—and I can scream louder than you can and I'll frighten you, I'll frighten you!"

He actually had stopped screaming because she had startled him so. The scream which had been coming almost choked him. The tears were streaming down his face and he shook all over.

"I can't stop!" he gasped and sobbed. "I can't—I can't!"

"You can!" shouted Mary. "Half that ails you is hysterics and temper—just hysterics—hysterics—hysterics!" and she stamped each time she said it.

"I felt the lump—I felt it," choked out Colin. "I knew I should. I shall have a hunch on my back and then I shall die," and he began to writhe again and turned on his face and sobbed and wailed but he didn't scream.

"You didn't feel a lump!" contradicted Mary fiercely. "If you did it was only a hysterical lump. Hysterics makes lumps. There's nothing the matter with your horrid back—nothing but hysterics! Turn over and let me look at it!"

She liked the word "hysterics" and felt somehow as if it had an effect on him. He was probably like herself and had never heard it before.

"Nurse," she commanded, "come here and show me his back this minute!"

The nurse, Mrs. Medlock and Martha had been standing huddled together near the door staring at her, their mouths half open. All three had gasped with fright more than once. The nurse came forward as if she were half afraid. Colin was heaving with great breathless sobs.

"Perhaps he—he won't let me," she hesitated in a low voice.

Colin heard her, however, and he gasped out between two sobs: "Sh—show her! She—she'll see then!"

It was a poor thin back to look at when it was bared. Every rib could be counted and every joint of the spine, though Mistress Mary did not count them as she bent over and examined them with a solemn savage little face. She looked so sour and old-fashioned that the nurse turned her head aside to hide the twitching of her mouth. There was just a minute's silence, for even Colin tried to hold his breath while Mary looked up and down his spine, and down and up, as intently as if she had been the great doctor from London.

"There's not a single lump there!" she said at last. "There's not a lump as big as a pin—except backbone lumps, and you can only feel them because you're thin. I've got backbone lumps myself, and they used to stick out as much as yours do, until I began to get fatter, and I am not fat enough yet to hide them. There's not a lump as big as a pin! If you ever say there is again, I shall laugh!"

No one but Colin himself knew what effect those crossly spoken childish words had on him. If he had ever had any one to talk to about his secret terrors—if he had ever dared to let himself ask questions—if he had had childish companions and had not lain on his back in the huge closed house, breathing an atmosphere heavy with the fears of people who were most of them ignorant and tired of him, he would have found out that most of his fright and illness was created by himself. But he had lain and thought of himself and his aches and weariness for hours and days and months and years. And now that an angry unsympathetic little girl insisted obstinately that he was not as ill as he thought he was he actually felt as if she might be speaking the truth.

"I didn't know," ventured the nurse, "that he thought he had a lump on his spine. His back is weak because he won't try to sit up. I could have told him there was no lump there."

Colin gulped and turned his face a little to look at her.

"C-could you?" he said pathetically.

"Yes, sir."

"There!" said Mary, and she gulped too.

Colin turned on his face again and but for his long-drawn broken breaths, which were the dying down of his storm of sobbing, he lay still for a minute, though great tears streamed down his face and wet the pillow. Actually the tears meant that a curious great relief had come to him. Presently he turned and looked at the nurse again and strangely enough he was not like a Rajah at all as he spoke to her.

"Do you think—I could—live to grow up?" he said.

## LENT WEEK 4

### *Chief of Sinners*

OPENING PRAYER
O Lord and Master of my life,
remove from me this languid spirit,
this grim demeanor, this petty
lust for power, and all this empty talk.
Endow Thy servant, instead,
with a chaste spirit, a humble
heart, longsuffering gentleness,
and genuine, unselfish love. . . .
—EPHRAIM OF SYRIA (fourth century)
adapted by Scott Cairns


SCRIPTURES
PSALM 51 | LAMENTATIONS 1:20–22 | 1 TIMOTHY 1:12–17 | LUKE 19:1–27


READINGS
"The Sinner" by GEORGE HERBERT
"Solar Ice" by PAUL MARIANI
"I am a little world made cunningly (Divine Meditations: V)"
by JOHN DONNE
"The Doubter's Prayer" by ANNE BRONTË
"Calcutta to Cannon Beach" by NATHANIEL LEE HANSEN
From *Crime and Punishment* by FYODOR DOSTOEVSKY


PERSONAL PRAYER AND REFLECTION

CLOSING PRAYER

. . . Yes, O Lord and King, grant
that I may confront my own offenses,
and remember not to judge my brother.
For You are—always and forever—blessed.
— EPHRAIM OF SYRIA (fourth century)
adapted by Scott Cairns

# READINGS

## The Sinner
GEORGE HERBERT (English, 1593–1633)

Lord, how I am all ague, when I seek
    What I have treasured in my memory!
    Since, if my soul make even with the week,
Each seventh note by right is due to thee.

I find there quarries of piled vanities,
    But shreds of holiness, that dare not venture
    To show their face, since cross to thy decrees:
There the circumference earth is, heaven the center.

In so much dregs the quintessence is small:
    The spirit and good extract of my heart
    Comes to about the many hundredth part.
Yet, Lord, restore thine image, hear my call:

    And though my hard heart scarce to thee can groan,
Remember that thou once didst write in stone.

————

## Solar Ice

PAUL MARIANI (Anglo-American, contemporary)

The sudden shock of what you really are.
Early March. The tentative return of afternoons.
Saturday, and Mass again. The four.
All about swelling buds on beech & ash
& maples. Crocuses & snowdrops
trilling. Four months impacted ice at last
receding from the north side of the house,
and bobbing robins back & soon, soon, red-
winged blackbirds strutting on the lawn.
Soon too the sweet familiar groundswell
of peepers in the marshes. Reason
enough to melt the frozen heart.

Father lifted the host above his head & prayed:
a small white sun around which everything
seemed to coalesce, cohere & choir. But
as I raised my head, the thought
of some old insult likewise reared
its head, and in that instant the arctic
hatred flared, shutting out my world
& spring, along with, yes, my lovely wife & sons,
a no & no & yet another no, until I caught
myself refuse the proffered gift of Love.

At once the host diminished to a tiny o:
an empty cipher, like some solar disc
imploding on itself. Only my precious
hate remained, the self-salt taste
of some old wound rubbed raw again,
a jagged O at the center of my world.
Ah, so this is it, I whistled through my teeth.

So this is hell, or some lovely ether
foretaste of it, alone at ninety north,
with darkness everywhere, & ice & ice
& ice & more ice on the way, and this
sweet abyss between myself & You.

———

### '*I am a little world made cunningly*'
#### (*Divine Meditations: V*)
JOHN DONNE (English, 1572–1631)

I am a little world made cunningly
Of elements, and an angelic sprite,
But black sin hath betrayed to endless night
My worlds both parts, and, oh, both parts must die.
You which beyond that heaven which was most high
Have found new spheres, and of new lands can write,
Pour new seas in mine eyes, that so I might
Drown my world with my weeping earnestly,
Or wash it, if it must be drowned no more:
But oh it must be burnt! alas the fire
Of lust and envy have burnt it heretofore,
And made it fouler; Let their flames retire,
And burn me O Lord, with a fiery zeal
Of thee and thy house, which doth in eating heal.

———

## The Doubter's Prayer

ANNE BRONTË (English, 1820–1849)

While faith is with me, I am blest;
It turns my darkest night to day;
But, while I clasp it to my breast,
I often feel it slide away. . . .

What shall I do if all my love,
My hopes, my toil, are cast away?
And if there be no God above
To hear and bless me when I pray?

Oh, help me, God! For thou alone
Canst my distracted soul relieve.
Forsake it not: it is thine own,
Though weak, yet longing to believe.

———

## Calcutta to Cannon Beach

NATHANIEL LEE HANSEN (Anglo-American, contemporary)

> *I have His darkness—I have His pain,—I have the terrible*
> *longing for God.*
> —Mother Teresa

That at times this future saint
could not sense her Lord while sweating

words with pen read as a revelation
to me, disclosed that she was human, too.

God's omnipresence still too far—boils, sores,
and scars too near, so faith meant treading

the waters of theology's raw mystery,
their paradox: belief is doubt

that we can know with certainty.
And so I cup the ocean with my hands,

though fingers leak, dry, then crack.
Yet for a moment, I can clutch the ocean

with my makeshift bowl, taste
the salt my everyday eyes cannot see.

———

FROM *Crime and Punishment*
FYODOR DOSTOEVSKY (Russian, 1821–1881)

[Editor's note: The murderer Raskolnikov—tormented, sickly, half mad
with grandiose visions of his own righteousness—takes an interest in
the family of Sonia, a young woman of great faith who is forced into
prostitution to provide for her consumptive stepmother, Katerina
Ivanovna, and siblings. Sonia, as yet unaware of Raskolnikov's guilt and
bewildered by his attentions to her family, nonetheless senses he is
morally and spiritually adrift.]

Five minutes passed. He still paced up and down the room
in silence, not looking at her. At last he went up to her;
his eyes glittered. He put his two hands on her shoulders and
looked straight into her tearful face. His eyes were hard, feverish
and piercing, his lips were twitching. All at once he bent down
quickly and dropping to the ground, kissed her foot. Sonia drew
back from him as from a madman. And certainly he looked like
a madman.

"What are you doing to me?" she muttered, turning pale, and a
sudden anguish clutched at her heart.

He stood up at once.

"I did not bow down to you, I bowed down to all the suffering of humanity," he said wildly and walked away to the window. "Listen," he added, turning to her a minute later. "I said just now to an insolent man that he was not worth your little finger... and that I did my sister honor making her sit beside you."

"Ach, you said that to them! And in her presence?" cried Sonia, frightened. "Sit down with me! An honor! Why, I'm . . . dishonorable. . . . Ah, why did you say that?"

"It was not because of your dishonor and your sin I said that of you, but because of your great suffering. But you are a great sinner, that's true," he added almost solemnly, "and your worst sin is that you have destroyed and betrayed yourself *for nothing*. Isn't that fearful? Isn't it fearful that you are living in this filth which you loathe so, and at the same time you know yourself (you've only to open your eyes) that you are not helping anyone by it, not saving anyone from anything? Tell me," he went on almost in a frenzy, "how this shame and degradation can exist in you side by side with other, opposite, holy feelings? It would be better, a thousand times better and wiser to leap into the water and end it all!"

"But what would become of them?" Sonia asked faintly, gazing at him with eyes of anguish, but not seeming surprised at his suggestion.

Raskolnikov looked strangely at her. He read it all in her face: so she must have had that thought already, perhaps many times, and earnestly she had thought out in her despair how to end it and so earnestly, that now she scarcely wondered at his suggestion. She had not even noticed the cruelty of his words. (The significance of his reproaches and his peculiar attitude to her shame she had, of course, not noticed either, and that, too, was clear to him.) But he saw how monstrously the thought of her disgraceful, shameful position was torturing her and had long tortured her. "What, what," he thought, "could hitherto have hindered her from putting an end to it?" Only then he realized what those poor little orphan children and that pitiful half-crazy Katerina Ivanovna, knocking her head against the wall in her consumption, meant for Sonia.

But, nevertheless, it was clear to him again that with her character and the amount of education she had after all received, she could not in any case remain so. He was still confronted by the question, how could she have remained so long in that position without going out of her mind, since she could not bring herself to jump into the water? Of course he knew that Sonia's position was an exceptional case, though unhappily not unique and not infrequent, indeed; but that very exceptionalness, her tinge of education, her previous life might, one would have thought, have killed her at the first step on that revolting path. What held her up—surely not depravity? All that infamy had obviously only touched her mechanically, not one drop of real depravity had penetrated to her heart; he saw that. He saw through her as she stood before him....

"There are three ways before her," he thought, "the canal, the madhouse, or . . . at last to sink into depravity which obscures the mind and turns the heart to stone."

The last idea was the most revolting, but he was a sceptic, he was young, abstract, and therefore cruel, and so he could not help believing that the last end was the most likely.

"But can that be true?" he cried to himself. "Can that creature who has still preserved the purity of her spirit be consciously drawn at last into that sink of filth and iniquity? Can the process already have begun? Can it be that she has only been able to bear it till now, because vice has begun to be less loathsome to her? No, no, that cannot be!" he cried, as Sonia had just before. "No, what has kept her from the canal till now is the idea of sin and they, the children. . . . And if she has not gone out of her mind . . . but who says she has not gone out of her mind? Is she in her senses? Can one talk, can one reason as she does? How can she sit on the edge of the abyss of loathsomeness into which she is slipping and refuse to listen when she is told of danger? Does she expect a miracle? No doubt she does. Doesn't that all mean madness?"

He stayed obstinately at that thought. He liked that explanation indeed better than any other. He began looking more intently at her.

"So you pray to God a great deal, Sonia?" he asked her.

Sonia did not speak; he stood beside her waiting for an answer.

"What should I be without God?" she whispered rapidly, forcibly, glancing at him with suddenly flashing eyes, and squeezing his hand.

"Ah, so that is it!" he thought.

"And what does God do for you?" he asked, probing her further.

Sonia was silent a long while, as though she could not answer. Her weak chest kept heaving with emotion.

"Be silent! Don't ask! You don't deserve!" she cried suddenly, looking sternly and wrathfully at him.

"That's it, that's it," he repeated to himself.

"He does everything," she whispered quickly, looking down again.

"That's the way out! That's the explanation," he decided, scrutinizing her with eager curiosity, with a new, strange, almost morbid feeling. He gazed at that pale, thin, irregular, angular little face, those soft blue eyes, which could flash with such fire, such stern energy, that little body still shaking with indignation and anger— and it all seemed to him more and more strange, almost impossible. "She is a religious maniac!" he repeated to himself.

# LENT WEEK 5

## *Raising the Dead*

OPENING PRAYER
Unsullied life thy servant grant
Who tunes his harp to sound thy praise,
And still my life shall hymn thy love,
And glory to the Father raise.
—Synesius (Greek, AD 375–430)

SCRIPTURES
Psalm 30 | Ezekiel 37:1–14 | 1 Corinthians 15:35–49 | John 11:17–44

READINGS
"Newness of Life" by Tania Runyan
"Spring Forward" by Abigail Carroll
"At the round earth's imagined corners (Divine Meditations: VII)"
by John Donne
"Death & Transfiguration" by Paul Mariani
"Inclement Sonnet" by Susanna Childress
From *Crime and Punishment* by Fyodor Dostoevsky

PERSONAL PRAYER AND REFLECTION

CLOSING PRAYER
You free us from the dread of death,
and make this life a door. You grant
our very flesh a fallow season,
then gather all at the last horn's blast.
You sow the earth with these our bodies,

shaped by Your own Hand. You bring
the harvest in, transforming death into
abundant life, all defect into beauty.
—MACRINA THE YOUNGER (Turkish, ca. 327–379)
adapted by Scott Cairns

✠

## READINGS

*Newness of Life*
TANIA RUNYAN (Anglo-American, contemporary)

> *South African man wakes after 21 hours in morgue fridge*

What cold salvation,
dragging fingernails
through the frost

of a half-dream
then waking
to a plastic cocoon.

The louder you scream
from your aluminum drawer
the more they believe

you're a ghost come
to haul them inside.
I feel your shivering

in my own bones,
stumble with you
into the vicious light.

Some burst alive
on the pyres of the Spirit.
Some blink open

slowly, alone, packed in ice:
*How did I get here?*
*I never knew I was dead.*

———

## Spring Forward

ABIGAIL CARROLL (Anglo-American, contemporary)

The crocuses have nudged themselves up
through the snow, have opened, never
   *are opening,*
always daring. Ephemeral prophets,

first of the sun's spring projects, purple-
throated chorus of *will-have-beens*—
   year after
year, their oracles outlast them. Cold's

empire has not yet been undone, but
the cardinals have begun to loudly declare
   its undoing,
which is as good as the thing itself, as good

as the gutters' wild running, the spilling
of rain down the tar-slick roof, the filling
   and pooling,
the annual re-schooling of earth

in the vernal properties of water. A bud
both is and is not a flower: furled flag,
   curled-up
tongue of summer, envelope of fire—

What is this world but a seed of desire
some dream-bent farmer sowed in a field
            waiting for
the end of winter, waiting to be getting on

with the business of timothy and clover?
Light sends itself, a missive from the future:
            it's shining,
a definite *shined*, a bold, unquestionable

*having shone*—this because of the paths
it travels, the distances it flies. The crocuses
            shiver; still
they will not be deterred from their singing,

from the sure and heady prospect of their
*having sung*. The notion of green has not
            yet occurred
to the ground—twig tips, bulbs, cattails,

bark: all stuck in a past perfect of gray—
but green *has* occurred to the sun. A kingdom
            is in
the making—and in the making has come.

———

### 'At the round earth's imagined corners'
*(Divine Meditations: VII)*
JOHN DONNE (English, 1572–1631)

At the round earth's imagined corners, blow
Your trumpets, angels, and arise, arise
From death, you numberless infinities
Of souls, and to your scattered bodies go,

All whom the flood did, and fire shall o'erthrow,
All whom war, dearth, age, agues, tyrannies,
Despair, law, chance, hath slain, and you whose eyes,
Shall behold God, and never taste death's woe.
But let them sleep, Lord, and me mourn a space,
For, if above all these, my sins abound,
'Tis late to ask abundance of thy grace,
When we are there; here on this lowly ground,
Teach me how to repent; for that's as good
As if thou hadst sealed my pardon, with thy blood.

―――

## Death & Transfiguration

PAUL MARIANI (Anglo-American, contemporary)

Down the precipitous switchbacks at eighty
the pokerfaced Palestinian cabby aims his Mercedes
while the three of us, ersatz pilgrims, blank-eyed, lurch,
and the droll Franciscan goes on about the Art Deco Church

of the Transfiguration crowning the summit of the Mount.
Up there I'd touched the damp stones of the old Crusader fount,
paced the thick walls, imagined Muslims circling below
on horseback, muleback, then ascending for the final blow.

A decent pasta and a dry wine, thanks to the Fratelli who run
the hostel at the site, followed by an even drier lecture in the sun-
drenched court, then back down to the glinting taxis, ready
to return us now to the same old, feverish, unsteady

world half a mile below. I thought of the old masters, so
many of them who had tried to ignite this scene: Angelico,
di Buoninsegna, Bellini, Perugino, the Frenchman John of Berry,
the Preobrazheniye (Russian, Novgorod, sixteenth century),

and thought at last of what Raphael had wrought. It was to be
his final work, commissioned for some French cathedral, his early
death at thirty-seven intervening. For those who only dream
of some vertiginous, longed-for transfiguration, he would seem

to hold out something magnanimous and large: the benzine brightness
of the Christ, eyes upraised in the atom flash of whiteness,
that body lifted up, cloud-suspended feet above the earth. There,
on either side, with the Tablets and the Book: Moses and Elijah.

Below, his fear-bedazzled friends: Peter, James, and John. And though
paint is only paint, we can almost hear the Father's words again, so
caught up in the vision was the artist: *This is my beloved Son,
on whom my favor rests. Listen to him.* Meanwhile, someone

in the lower half of the picture is gesturing toward the transfigured
Christ. He is part of the curious and anxious crowd
that surrounds the epileptic youth, whose eyes, like Christ's, are wide,
but wide with seizure like some frenzied Sibyl's: the great divide

that separates him from the others, as if he understood the same strange
thing Raphael came to see as he composed this scene: that the deranged
youth has somehow come upon a mystery. Like us, he has been bound
round with fear, and only the One descending as he comes can sound

those depths of cosmic light and dark, in which the young man
writhes honeystruck in death, though he will—the gospel says—be
    raised again
to health and to his father, in this prologue to the resurrection.
That's it, then, it would seem: first the old fears descending, then dejection

and the dunning sameness in the daily going round and round of things.
Then a light like ten thousand suns that flames the brain and brings
another kind of death with it, and then—once more—the daily round
again. But changed now by what the blind beseeching eye has found.

———

## *Inclement Sonnet*
SUSANNA CHILDRESS (Anglo-American, contemporary)

Tell me snow is falling on the willows now, fat, full, unhurried,
for our bald neighbor-boy sleeps, his dark body beneath
a blanket knit brilliantly blue, his body wilted with
neuroblastoma. Here on the couch, Emmy holds his head

while I wonder at what's sent from above, what we'd believe
drifts down during these months of ice, so far north we need
Easter to end winter for us—not Eostre, Teutonic myth,
vernal equinox; not eggs, red-iris bunnies, beribboned

sweets. Tell me what comes next: tires spinning, marrow
aspirating, gladiolus whispering *when, when,* Wednesday
ashing our brows and, for each, some coruscating stretch, most

Fridays not so good after all. Last week he told his mum, *I get a new
body if I go to heaven.* Tell me it's coming soon, Pascha Sunday,
that, as they lift, our arms will ache, will awaken, with all we've lost.

———

## FROM *Crime and Punishment*
FYODOR DOSTOEVSKY (Russian, 1821–1881)

> [Editor's note: Raskolnikov, who has murdered an old woman and her sister
> Lizaveta, continues his visit with the faithful but fallen prostitute Sonia.]

There was a book lying on the chest of drawers. He had noticed
it every time he paced up and down the room. Now he took
it up and looked at it. It was the New Testament in the Russian
translation. It was bound in leather, old and worn.

"Where did you get that?" he called to her across the room.

She was still standing in the same place, three steps from the table.

"It was brought me," she answered, with seeming reluctance, not looking at him.

"Who brought it?"

"Lizaveta; I asked her for it."

"Lizaveta! strange!" he thought.

Everything about Sonia seemed to him stranger and more wonderful every moment. He carried the book to the candle and began to turn over the pages.

"Where is the story of Lazarus?" he asked suddenly.

Sonia looked obstinately at the ground and would not answer. She was standing sideways to the table.

"Where is the raising of Lazarus? Find it for me, Sonia."

She stole a glance at him.

"You are not looking in the right place. . . . It's in the fourth gospel," she whispered sternly, without looking at him.

"Find it and read it to me," he said. He sat down with his elbow on the table, leaned his head on his hand and looked away sullenly, prepared to listen.

"In three weeks' time they'll welcome me in the madhouse! I shall be there if I am not in a worse place," he muttered to himself.

Sonia heard Raskolnikov's request distrustfully and moved with hesitation to the table.

"Haven't you read it?" she asked, looking up at him across the table. Her voice became sterner and sterner.

"Long ago. . . . When I was at school. Read!"

"And haven't you heard it in church?"

"I . . . haven't been. Do you often go?"

"N-no," whispered Sonia.

Raskolnikov's face twisted in a smile.

"I understand. . . . And you won't go to your father's funeral to-morrow?"

"Yes, I shall. I was at church last week, too. . . . I had a requiem service."

"For whom?"

"For Lizaveta. She was killed with an axe."

His nerves were more and more strained. His head began to go round.

"Were you friends with Lizaveta?"

"Yes. . . . She was good . . . she used to come . . . not often . . . she couldn't. . . . We used to read together and . . . talk. She will see God."

The last phrase sounded strange in his ears. And here was something new again: the mysterious meetings with Lizaveta and both of them—religious maniacs.

"I shall be a religious maniac myself soon!" he thought. "It's infectious!" "Read!" he cried, insistent and irritable.

Sonia still hesitated. Her heart was throbbing. She hardly dared to read to him. He looked almost with exasperation at the "unhappy lunatic."

"What for? You don't believe, do you? . . ." she whispered softly, almost panting.

"Read! I want you to," he persisted. "You used to read to Lizaveta."

Sonia opened the book and found the place. Her hands were shaking, her voice failed her. Twice she tried to begin and could not bring out the first syllable.

"Now a certain man was sick named Lazarus of Bethany . . ." she forced herself at last to read, but at the third word her voice broke like an overstrained string. There was a catch in her breath.

Raskolnikov saw in part why Sonia could not bring herself to read to him; and the more he saw this, the more roughly and irritably he insisted on her doing so. He understood only too well how painful it was for her to betray and unveil all that was her *own*. He understood that these feelings really were her *secret treasure*, which she had kept perhaps for years, perhaps from childhood, while she lived with an unhappy father and a distracted stepmother crazed by grief, in the midst of starving children and unseemly abuse and reproaches. But at the same time he knew now and knew for certain that, although it filled her with dread and suffering, yet she had a tormenting desire to read and to read to *him* that he might hear it, and to read *now* whatever might come of it!... He read this in her eyes; he could see it in her intense emotion. She mastered herself, controlled the spasm in her throat, and went on reading the eleventh chapter of St. John. . . .

. . .Raskolnikov turned and looked at her with emotion. Yes, he had known it! She was trembling in a real physical fever. He had expected it. She was getting near the story of the greatest miracle and a feeling of immense triumph came over her. Her voice rang out like a bell; triumph and joy gave it power. The lines danced before her eyes, but she knew what she was reading by heart. At the last verse "Could not this Man which opened the eyes of the blind . . ." dropping her voice she passionately reproduced the doubt, the reproach and censure of the blind disbelieving Jews, who in another moment would fall at His feet as though struck by thunder, sobbing and believing. . . . "And *he, he*—too, is blinded and unbelieving, he, too, will hear, he, too, will believe, yes, yes! At once, now," was what she was dreaming, and she was quivering with happy anticipation.

"Jesus therefore again groaning in Himself cometh to the grave. It was a cave, and a stone lay upon it.

"Jesus said, Take ye away the stone. Martha, the sister of him that was dead, saith unto Him, Lord by this time he stinketh: for he hath been dead four days."

She laid emphasis on the word *four*.

"Jesus saith unto her, Said I not unto thee that if thou wouldest believe, thou shouldest see the glory of God?

"Then they took away the stone from the place where the dead was laid. And Jesus lifted up His eyes and said, Father, I thank Thee that Thou hast heard Me.

"And I knew that Thou hearest Me always; but because of the people which stand by I said it, that they may believe that Thou hast sent Me.

"And when He thus had spoken, He cried with a loud voice, Lazarus, come forth.

"And he that was dead came forth."

(She read loudly, cold and trembling with ecstasy, as though she were seeing it before her eyes.)

"Bound hand and foot with graveclothes; and his face was bound about with a napkin. Jesus saith unto them, Loose him and let him go.

"Then many of the Jews which came to Mary and had seen the things which Jesus did believed on Him."

She could read no more, closed the book and got up from her chair quickly.

"That is all about the raising of Lazarus," she whispered severely and abruptly, and turning away she stood motionless, not daring to raise her eyes to him. Her feverish trembling still continued. The candle-end was flickering out in the battered candlestick, dimly lighting up in the poverty-stricken room the murderer and the harlot who had so strangely encountered each other in the reading of the eternal book.

# PALM SUNDAY

## *The Jubilant Crowd*

### OPENING PRAYER

Haste to me, Lord, when this fool-heart of mine
Begins to gnaw itself with selfish craving;
Or, like a foul thing scarcely worth the saving,
Swoln up with wrath, desirest vengeance fine.
Haste, Lord, to help, when reason favors wrong;
Haste when thy soul, the high-born thing divine,
Is torn by passion's raving, maniac throng.
— GEORGE MACDONALD (Scottish, 1824–1905)

### SCRIPTURES

PSALM 122 | ZECHARIAH 9:9–12 | 1 CORINTHIANS 15:30–34 |
MARK 11:1–11

### READINGS

"Cachoeira" by MARILYN NELSON
"Sunday" by HANNAH FAITH NOTESS
"The blind suppliant (Luke 18:39)" by RICHARD CRASHAW
"He who would be great among you…" by LUCI SHAW
From *A Tale of Two Cities* by CHARLES DICKENS

### PERSONAL PRAYER AND REFLECTION

CLOSING PRAYER

lord
spread wide your arms
and protect us
from the multitude of your guardians
stand by those who wander
who've not lost the gift of hearing
and listen within their solitude
stand by those too
who stay and wait for you
— SAID (Iranian, contemporary)

## READINGS

### *Cachoeira*
MARILYN NELSON (African-American, contemporary)

[Editor's note: Nelson recounts her tour with companions to Brazil in
a Chaucer-like cycle of poems, of which the following is one.]

We slept, woke, breakfasted, and met the man
we'd hired as a tour guide, with a van
and driver, for the day. We were to drive
to Cachoeria, where the sisters live:
the famous Sisterhood of the Good Death,
founded by former slaves in the nineteenth
century. "Negroes of the Higher Ground,"
they called themselves, the governesses who founded the Sisterhood as a way to serve the poor.
Their motto, *"Aiye Orun,"*[10] names the door
between this world and the other, kept ajar.
They teach that death is relative: We rise

to dance again. Locally canonized,
they lead quiet, celibate, nunnish lives,
joining after they've been mothers and wives,
at between fifty and seventy years of age:
a sisterhood of sages in matronage.

We drove on Salvador's four-lane boulevards,
past unpainted cement houses, and billboards,
and pedestrians wearing plastic shoes,
and little shops, and streets, and avenues,
a park, a mall…Our guide was excellent:
fluent in English, and intelligent,
willing to answer questions patiently
and to wait out our jokes. The history
of Salvador flew past. At Tororo
we slowed as much as the traffic would allow,
to see the Orixas[11] dancing on the lake
in their bright skirts. The road we took
sped past high-rise apartment neighborhoods,
then scattered shacks, then nothing but deep woods
of trees I didn't recognize and lands
that seemed to be untouched by human hands.
We stopped in a village, where it was market day.
We walked among the crowds, taller than they
and kilos heavier, tasting jackfruit
and boiled peanuts, embraced by absolute,
respectful welcome, like visiting gods
whose very presence is good news. Our guide
suggested a rest stop. We were sipping Coke
when a man came into the shop and quietly spoke
to our guide, who translated his request:
Would we come to his nightclub, be his guests?
We didn't understand, but shrugged and went

a few doors down the street. "What does he want?"
we asked. The club hadn't been opened yet;
by inviting us in, the owner hoped to get
our blessings for it. Which we humbly gave:
visiting rich American descendants of slaves.

For hours we drove through a deep wilderness,
laughing like children on a field-trip bus.
We made a side trip to the family home
of Bahia's favorite daughter and son,
the Velosos, Bethania and Caetano,
in the small town of Santo Amaro.
The greenery flew by until the descent
into a river valley. There we went
to a nice little restaurant to dine
on octopus stew, rice, manioc, and wine.
Then we crossed a rickety bridge behind a dray
drawn by a donkey, and wended our way,
at last, to Cachoeira, an old town
of colonial buildings, universally tan
and shuttered, darkly lining narrow streets.
A tethered rooster pecked around our feet
in the souvenir shop. At the convent
I wondered what the statues really meant:
Was it Mary, or was it Yemanja[12]
in the chapel, blue-robed, over the altar?
Was it Mary on the glass-enclosed bier,
her blue robe gold-embroidered, pearls in her hair,
or was it the Orixa of the sea?
There were no Sisters around for us to see;
they were in solitude, preparing for the Feast
of the Assumption, when the Virgin passed
painlessly from this world into the next,

*Aiye* to *Orun*. Posters showed them decked
out for their big Assumption Day parade,
big, handsome mamas wearing Orixa beads,
white turbans and blouses, red shawls, black skirts.
The man in their gift shop was an expert
on the Sisters' long struggle to find a way
to serve the Christian Church and Candomblé.[13]
The eldest Sister is called "the Perpetual Judge":
every seventh year, she becomes the bridge
on which the Virgin Mary crosses back,
sorrowing love incarnate in a black
ninety-odd-year-old woman facing death
and saying *Magnifica*t with every breath.

We drove out of the valley looking back
on lightbulbs which intensified the thick,
incomprehensible, mysterious
darkness of the unknown. Grown serious
and silent in our air-conditioned van,
we rode back into the quotidian.

———

## Sunday
HANNAH FAITH NOTESS (Anglo-American, contemporary)

After the parade, the tired donkey
wanders back to her stall.
Among the bruised feathery branches,
a dog licks at a half-eaten snack
wrapped in a leaf, and the palms,
whose boughs are done being cut down,
begin again to whisper
their fragile green music.

Mud crusts and dries
on abandoned, trampled cloaks,
and the women carry some of them
down to the water for washing. *He seemed
like a nice man*, they tell each other.
He came from the country.

Across the city, the man
who had *a strong face, a kind face*,
is telling a story with his hands,
and in the lamplight
the wise and foolish virgins
cast shadows on the wall.

Tomorrow his hands will wither
a fig tree and overturn tables.
The temple veil will start
to stretch and fray. But on this street,
as night falls over the city, and the women
shoulder their dripping burdens
up the hill, the mutter of voices
at the well is only gossip,
and the wail rising in the air
is only a child's cry, hungry and thin.

––––

*The blind suppliant (Luke 18:39)*
RICHARD CRASHAW (English, 1612–1649)

Silence, silence, O vile crowd;
Yea, I will now cry aloud:
He comes near, Who is to me
Light and life and liberty.

Silence seek ye? yes, I'll be
Silent when He speaks to me,
He my Hope; ah, meek and still,
I shall 'bide His holy will.
O crowd, ye it may surprise,
But His voice holdeth my eyes:
O have pity on my night,
By the day that gives glad light;
O have pity on my night,
By the day would lose its light,
If it gat[14] not of Thee sight;
O have pity on my night,
By day of faith upspringing bright;
That day within my soul that burns,
And for eyes' day unto Thee turns.
Lord, O Lord, give me this day,
Nor do Thou take that away.

———

*"He who would be great among you..."*
LUCI SHAW (naturalized U.S. citizen, contemporary)

*Matthew 20:26*

You, whose birth broke all the social and biological rules—
son of the poor who was worshiped as a king—
you were the kind who used a new math to multiply
bread, fish, faith. You practiced a radical sociology:
rehabilitating call girls and con men.
You valued women and other minority groups.
A family practitioner, you specialized in heart transplants.

Creator, healer, shepherd, storyteller,
innovator, weather-maker, exorcist, iconoclast,
seeker, seer, motive-sifter, you were always beyond, above us,
ahead of your time, and ours.
And we would like to be like you!
Bold as the Boanerges we hear ourselves demand:
"Admit us to your inner circle.
Grant us degree in all the liberal arts of heaven."

Why our belligerence? Why does this whiff of fame
and power smell so sweet?
Why must we compete
to be first? Have we forgotten
how you took, so simply, cool water
and a towel for our feet?

———

## FROM *A Tale of Two Cities*
Charles Dickens (English, 1812–1870)

[Editor's note: Not long before the French Revolution, a young aristocrat named Evremonde disavows his family's wicked heritage and begins a new life in England as Charles Darnay. There he meets a former French prisoner, Doctor Manette, and marries Manette's beautiful daughter Lucie. The two start a family in London, but eventually the revolution begins; and Darnay finds himself called back to France in an effort to save an old family servant, who is wrongly imprisoned in the Bastille. Darnay is himself imprisoned and nearly sentenced to death, but through the efforts of Doctor Manette—who has become a national hero—Darnay is acquitted. For now.]

Then, began one of those extraordinary scenes with which the populace sometimes gratified their fickleness, or their better impulses towards generosity and mercy, or which they regarded as some set-off against their swollen account of cruel rage. No man can decide now to which of these motives such extraordinary scenes were referable; it is probable, to a blending of all the three, with the second predominating. No sooner was the acquittal pronounced, than tears were shed as freely as blood at another time, and such fraternal embraces were bestowed upon the prisoner by as many of both sexes as could rush at him, that after his long and unwholesome confinement he was in danger of fainting from exhaustion; none the less because he knew very well, that the very same people, carried by another current, would have rushed at him with the very same intensity, to rend him to pieces and strew him over the streets.

His removal, to make way for other accused persons who were to be tried, rescued him from these caresses for the moment. Five were to be tried together, next, as enemies of the Republic, forasmuch as they had not assisted it by word or deed. So quick was the Tribunal to compensate itself and the nation for a chance lost, that these five came down to him before he left the place, condemned to die within twenty-four hours. The first of them told him so, with the customary prison sign of Death—a raised finger—and they all added in words, "Long live the Republic!"

The five had had, it is true, no audience to lengthen their proceedings, for when he and Doctor Manette emerged from the gate, there was a great crowd about it, in which there seemed to be every face he had seen in Court—except two, for which he looked in vain. On his coming out, the concourse made at him anew, weeping, embracing, and shouting, all by turns and all together, until the very tide of the river on the bank of which the mad scene was acted, seemed to run mad, like the people on the shore.

They put him into a great chair they had among them, and which they had taken either out of the Court itself, or one of its rooms or passages. Over the chair they had thrown a red flag, and to the back of it they had bound a pike with a red cap on its top. In this car of triumph, not even the Doctor's entreaties could prevent his being carried to his home on men's shoulders, with a confused sea of red caps heaving about him, and casting up to sight from the stormy deep such wrecks of faces, that he more than once misdoubted his mind being in confusion, and that he was in the tumbril on his way to the Guillotine.

In wild dreamlike procession, embracing whom they met and pointing him out, they carried him on. Reddening the snowy streets with the prevailing Republican color, in winding and tramping through them, as they had reddened them below the snow with a deeper dye, they carried him thus into the courtyard of the building where he lived. Her father had gone on before, to prepare her, and when her husband stood upon his feet, she dropped insensible in his arms.

As he held her to his heart and turned her beautiful head between his face and the brawling crowd, so that his tears and her lips might come together unseen, a few of the people fell to dancing. Instantly, all the rest fell to dancing, and the courtyard overflowed with the Carmagnole.[15] Then, they elevated into the vacant chair a young woman from the crowd to be carried as the Goddess of Liberty, and then swelling and overflowing out into the adjacent streets, and along the river's bank, and over the bridge, the Carmagnole absorbed them every one and whirled them away.

After grasping the Doctor's hand, as he stood victorious and proud before him; after grasping the hand of Mr. Lorry, who came panting in breathless from his struggle against the waterspout of the Carmagnole; after kissing little Lucie, who was lifted up to clasp her arms round his neck; and after embracing the ever zealous and faithful Pross who lifted her; he took his wife in his arms, and carried her up to their rooms.

"Lucie! My own! I am safe."

"O dearest Charles, let me thank God for this on my knees as I have prayed to Him."

They all reverently bowed their heads and hearts. When she was again in his arms, he said to her:

"And now speak to your father, dearest. No other man in all this France could have done what he has done for me."

She laid her head upon her father's breast, as she had laid his poor head on her own breast, long, long ago. He was happy in the return he had made her, he was recompensed for his suffering, he was proud of his strength. "You must not be weak, my darling," he remonstrated; "don't tremble so. I have saved him."

## HOLY MONDAY

# *Things Fall Apart*

### OPENING PRAYER

Thou tarriest, while I die,
And fall to nothing: thou dost reign,
And rule on high,
While I remain
In bitter grief: yet am I styled
Thy child…

—GEORGE HERBERT (English, 1593–1633)

### SCRIPTURES

PSALM 53 | EZEKIEL 7:1–12 | ROMANS 1:18–25 | MARK 11:12–19

### READINGS

"Six Holy Week Triolets" by L. N. ALLEN
"The People of Laish" by MARY F. C. PRATT
"The Second Coming" by WILLIAM BUTLER YEATS
"Song for the End of Time" by DANA GIOIA
From *Purple Hibiscus* by CHIMAMANDA NGOZI ADICHIE

### PERSONAL PRAYER AND REFLECTION

### CLOSING PRAYER

. . . My love, my sweetness, hear!
By these thy feet, at which my heart
Lies all the year,
Pluck out thy dart,

And heal my troubled breast which cries,
Which dies.
—GEORGE HERBERT (English, 1593–1633)

## READINGS

### Six Holy Week Triolets
L. N. ALLEN (Anglo-American, contemporary)

#### Monday

*After he cursed the fig tree,*
*it withered away to its roots.*
Faith can throw mountains into the sea.
After he cursed the fig tree
he told his disciples *Trust in me,*
*pray, walk the path, preach the truth.*
After he cursed the fig tree
it withered away to its roots.

#### Tuesday

*Unless a grain of wheat falls to the earth and dies*
*it remains just a single grain.*
Only the fallen and buried can rise.
Unless a grain of wheat falls to the earth and dies
it cannot grow and multiply
and it thirsts, although drowned in rain.
Unless a grain of wheat falls to the earth and dies
it remains just a single grain.

## Wednesday

*Walk while you have the light*
*so the darkness may not overtake you.*
Believe in the light.
Walk while you have the light.
Become children of the light.
For a little longer, the light is with you.
Walk while you have the light
so the darkness may not overtake you.

## Thursday

*"Truly I tell you, one of you will betray me."*
*Each of the twelve cried, "Surely, not I?"*
"As it was for the fig tree, it will be for the spy—
Truly I tell you, one of you will betray me—
Take, eat, this is my body."
He broke the bread, he passed the wine.
"Truly I tell you, one of you will betray me."
Each of the twelve cried, "Surely, not I?"

## Friday

*Where I am going, you cannot follow now,*
*but you will follow afterward,*
with prayers and sighs too deep for words.
Where I am going, you cannot follow now,
yet though a hundred pounds of myrrh and aloe
are between us, I will not leave you orphaned.
Where I am going, you cannot follow now.
But you will follow afterward.

Saturday

*To set the mind on the flesh is death.*
*Set the mind on the Spirit for life and peace.*
Note where the sun rises, not where it sets.
To set the mind on the flesh is death.
Pray to Abba for hope. Not for breath,
but for mercy, forgiveness, release.
To set the mind on the flesh is death.
Set the mind on the Spirit for life and peace.

———

## The People of Laish
MARY F. C. PRATT (Anglo-American, contemporary)

> *The Danites came to Laish, to a people quiet and unsuspecting:*
> *and smote them with the edge of the sword, and burnt the city*
> *with fire. And there was no deliverer....*
> — Judges 18:27–28

In the morning, a woman walked to her field,
stopped, puzzled by moving shadows,
a far rattle of sound she'd never heard.
In the crackling ruin of that night
jackals circled the city,
waiting for the flames to die.

We create gods in our image.
The god of Dan, glorious in battle,
adept with fire;
the god of Laish, quiet and unsuspecting,
no deliverer.

The one time god created itself in our image
we didn't like it:
too messy, too common.
Bones, and a great deal of blood.
Not the sort of deliverer anyone wanted.

I walked early today down the usual road:
dark woods on my left,
cut hayfields on my right.
Against the blue bulk of mountains,
one wisp of cloud drifting up,
blowing apart in the sunrise.

———

## The Second Coming
WILLIAM BUTLER YEATS (Irish, 1865–1939)

Turning and turning in the widening gyre
The falcon cannot hear the falconer;
Things fall apart; the center cannot hold;
Mere anarchy is loosed upon the world,
The blood-dimmed tide is loosed, and everywhere
The ceremony of innocence is drowned;
The best lack all conviction, while the worst
Are full of passionate intensity.

Surely some revelation is at hand;
Surely the Second Coming is at hand.
The Second Coming! Hardly are those words out
When a vast image out of *Spiritus Mundi*
Troubles my sight: a waste of desert sand;
A shape with lion body and the head of a man,
A gaze blank and pitiless as the sun,

Is moving its slow thighs, while all about it
Reel shadows of the indignant desert birds.
The darkness drops again; but now I know
That twenty centuries of stony sleep
Were vexed to nightmare by a rocking cradle,
And what rough beast, its hour come round at last,
Slouches towards Bethlehem to be born?

———

## Song for the End of Time
DANA GIOIA (Anglo-American, contemporary)

The hanged man laughs by the garden wall,
And the hands of the clock have stopped at the hour.
The cathedral angels are starting to fall,
And the bells ring themselves in the gothic tower.

Lock up your money and go bolt the door,
And don't dare look yourself in the eye.
Pray on your knees or cry on the floor
Or stare at the stars as they fall from the sky.

You may say that you're sorry for all that you've done,
You may swear on your honor and protest with tears.
But the moon is burning under the sun,
And nothing you do will stop what appears.

———

## FROM *Purple Hibiscus*
CHIMAMANDA NGOZI ADICHIE (Nigerian-American, contemporary)

[Editor's note: Adichie's narrator, a fifteen-year-old girl named
Kambili, lives in a household of devastating contrasts. Her father is a

successful businessman in Enugu, Nigeria, revered for his charitable giving in their local Catholic parish; and he yet violently punishes his wife and children when they fail to live up to his extreme religious expectations. The story begins with a deliberate echo of African writer Chinua Achebe's best-known novel, *Things Fall Apart*: "Things started to fall apart at home when my brother, Jaja, did not go to communion. . . ." Only as the story progresses do we begin to learn how significant are the events of this opening scene.]

J aja, you did not go to communion," Papa said quietly, almost a question.

Jaja stared at the missal on the table as though he were addressing it. "The wafer gives me bad breath."

I stared at Jaja. Had something come loose in his head? Papa insisted we call it the host because "host" came close to capturing the essence, the sacredness of Christ's body. "Wafer" was too secular, wafer was what one of Papa's factories made—chocolate wafer, banana wafer, what people bought their children to give them a treat better than biscuits.

"And the priest keeps touching my mouth and it nauseates me," Jaja said. He knew I was looking at him, that my shocked eyes begged him to seal his mouth, but he did not look at me.

"It is the body of our Lord." Papa's voice was low, very low. His face looked swollen already, with pus-tipped rashes spread across every inch, but it seemed to be swelling even more. "You cannot stop receiving the body of our Lord. It is death, you know that."

"Then I will die." Fear had darkened Jaja's eyes to the color of coal tar, but he looked Papa in the face now. "Then I will die, Papa."

Papa looked around the room quickly, as if searching for proof that something had fallen from the high ceiling, something he had never thought would fall. He picked up the missal and flung it across the room, toward Jaja. It missed Jaja completely, but it hit the glass étagerè, which Mama polished often. It cracked the top shelf, swept the beige, finger-size ceramic figurines of ballet dancers in various contorted postures to the hard floor and then landed after them. Or rather it landed on their many pieces. It lay there, a huge leatherbound missal that contained the readings for all three cycles of the church year.

Jaja did not move. Papa swayed from side to side. I stood at the door, watching them. The ceiling fan spun round and round, and the light bulbs attached to it clinked against one another. Then Mama came in, her rubber slippers making *slap-slap* sounds on the marble floor. She had changed from her sequined Sunday wrapper and the blouse with puffy sleeves. Now she had a plain tie-dye wrapper tied loosely around her waist and that white T-shirt she wore every other day. It was a souvenir from a spiritual retreat she and Papa had attended; the words GOD IS LOVE crawled over her sagging breasts. She stared at the figurine pieces on the floor and then knelt and started to pick them up with her bare hands.

The silence was broken only by the whir of the ceiling fan as it sliced through the still air. Although our spacious dining room gave way to an even wider living room, I felt suffocated. The off-white walls with the framed photos of Grandfather were narrowing, bearing down on me. Even the glass dining table was moving toward me.

"*Nne, ngwa.* Go and change," Mama said to me, startling me although her Igbo words were low and calming. In the same breath, without pausing, she said to Papa, "Your tea is getting cold," and to Jaja, "Come and help me, *biko.*"

Papa sat down at the table and poured his tea from the china tea set with pink flowers on the edges. I waited for him to ask Jaja and me to take a sip, as he always did. A love sip, he called it, because you shared the little things you loved with the people you loved. Have a love sip, he would say, and Jaja would go first. Then I would hold the cup with both hands and raise it to my lips. One sip. The tea was always too hot, always burned my tongue, and if lunch was something peppery, my raw tongue suffered. But it didn't matter, because I knew that when the tea burned my tongue, it burned Papa's love into me. But Papa didn't say, "Have a love sip"; he didn't say anything as I watched him raise the cup to his lips.

Jaja knelt beside Mama, flattened the church bulletin he held into a dustpan, and placed a jagged ceramic piece on it. "Careful, Mama, or those pieces will cut your fingers," he said.

# Costly Betrayals

### OPENING PRAYER
lord,
make room
for the rebellious one i am
for my angerless hands
for my selective loyalty
that betrays everything
except dreams and prayers
—SAID (Iranian, contemporary)

### SCRIPTURES
PSALM 41 | 2 SAMUEL 12:1–14 | ROMANS 2:1–11 |
MARK 11:20–25; 14:1–11

### READINGS
"The Contemplative Life" by MARILYN NELSON
"Foreknowledge" by JEANNE MURRAY WALKER
"The Coronet" by ANDREW MARVELL
"The Look" by ELIZABETH BARRETT BROWNING
"The Meaning of The Look" by ELIZABETH BARRETT BROWNING
"Passionate Sins" by PAUL J. WILLIS
From *The Complete Father Brown: The Chief Mourner of Marne*
by G. K. CHESTERTON

### PERSONAL PRAYER AND REFLECTION

CLOSING PRAYER
Thou thrice denied, yet thrice beloved,
    Watch by thine own forgiven friend;
In sharpest perils faithful proved,
    Let his soul love thee to the end.
— JOHN KEBLE (English, 1792–1866)

READINGS

## The Contemplative Life

MARILYN NELSON (African-American, contemporary)

Abba Jacob said:
Contemplation is both the highest act
of being human, and humanity's highest language.
If the language of things reaches beyond things
to designate the Absolute,
the silent interior mantra
bespeaks a profound communion
with that Someone further than ourselves—
and communion within
ourselves, for the two go together.
When we meditate, we enter
paschal mystery, the frontier between death and life.
Egyptian mythology has a wonderful image
of the pass from life to death: a great ship
which bears us to eternity. Charon
is the great passer of Greek mythology,
helping souls cross the River Styx from life to death.
Christianity turns it around: Christ
is the greatest passer, helping us pass

from death to life.
Contemplative life is always making the passage
from death to life, from humanity to divinity.
It is always taking the risk of being human.

There is an extraordinary message from the grave
as to what it takes to be human: a letter
from a Cistercian monk, one of seven
who had their throats cut
by Muslim fundamentalist terrorists
in their monastery in the mountains of Algeria
about ten years ago. Their prior
left a letter, just in case:
they knew it was probably coming,
they knew they were at great risk.
The letter was found and published
Here is how it ends:

*To the one who will have killed me:*

*and also you, Friend of my final moment,*
*who would not be aware*
*of what you are doing,*
*yet, this: Thank you.*
*For in you, too,*
*I see the face of God.*

Abba Jacob wiped his eyes.
Interval of birdsong from the veranda.

He's seeing not an abstract God,
but a God who has assumed a face,
a God who shows him this face
in every one of those Muslim brothers and sisters,
including the one who kills him.

Contemplative life has no frontiers.
And it is the heritage of all humanity.
Through contemplation we enter
into communion with everybody.
And this leads to service.
But that's a subject
for another day.

––––

## Foreknowledge
JEANNE MURRAY WALKER (Anglo-American, contemporary)

I think he planned it, sort of, from the start,
whether he knew they'd choose the fruit or not.
He scattered hints around the garden, what to do
in case they got themselves kicked out. A shirt
of fur around the lamb. The stream converting
water into syllables. Bamboo pipes.
The caps of mushrooms round as wheels.
Bluebirds composing tunes. He knew nothing
they started later would be new. Except he
didn't factor in the thorns, how they would smart
as Adam—leaving—drove one through his foot.
How clever Romans would invent a crown.
He didn't figure weeds could break his heart.

––––

## The Coronet
ANDREW MARVELL (English, 1621–1678)

When for the Thorns with which I long, too long,
With many a piercing wound,

My Savior's head have crown'd,
I seek with Garlands to redress that Wrong:
Through every Garden, every Mead,
I gather flow'rs (my fruits are only flow'rs)
Dismantling all the fragrant Towers
That once adorn'd my Shepherdess's head.
And now when I have summ'd up all my store,
Thinking (so I my self deceive)
So rich a Chaplet thence to weave
As never yet the king of Glory wore:
Alas I find the Serpent old
That, twining in his speckled breast,
About the flow'rs disguis'd does fold,
With wreaths of Fame and Interest.
Ah, foolish Man, that would'st debase with them,
And mortal Glory, Heaven's Diadem!
But thou who only could'st the Serpent tame,
Either his slipp'ry knots at once untie,
And disentangle all his winding Snare:
Or shatter too with him my curious frame:
And let these wither, so that he may die,
Though set with Skill and chosen out with Care.
That they, while thou on both their Spoils doest tread,
May crown thy Feet, that could not crown thy Head.

———

## The Look

ELIZABETH BARRETT BROWNING (English, 1806–1861)

The Savior looked on Peter. Ay, no word,
No gesture of reproach; the Heavens serene
Though heavy with armed justice, did not lean

Their thunders that way: the forsaken Lord
Looked only, on the traitor. None record
What that look was, none guess; for those who have seen
Wronged lovers loving through a death-pang keen,
Or pale-cheeked martyrs smiling to a sword,
Have missed Jehovah at the judgment-call.
And Peter, from the height of blasphemy—
'I never knew this man'—did quail and fall
As knowing straight THAT GOD; and turned free
And went out speechless from the face of all
And filled the silence, weeping bitterly.

———

## The Meaning of The Look

ELIZABETH BARRETT BROWNING (English, 1806–1861)

I think that look of Christ might seem to say—
"Thou Peter! art thou then a common stone
Which I at last must break my heart upon
For all God's charge to his high angels may
Guard my foot better? Did I yesterday
Wash thy feet, my beloved, that they should run
Quick to deny me 'neath the morning sun?
And do thy kisses, like the rest, betray?
The cock crows coldly.—GO, and manifest
A late contrition, but no bootless fear!
For when thy final need is dreariest,
Thou shalt not be denied, as I am here;
My voice to God and angels shall attest,
Because I KNOW this man, let him be clear."

———

## Passionate Sins

PAUL J. WILLIS (Anglo-American, contemporary)

> —*Luke 22*

Would I betray you with a kiss
    deny you with a word
        accuse you from your lips?

Surely I would
    and have
        and will

As the cock crows on
    in the dawn
        of grace.

———

FROM *The Complete Father Brown: The Chief Mourner of Marne*
G. K. CHESTERTON (English, 1874–1936)

[Editor's note: After an oddly-assorted group of day-trippers gets rained out of a picnic near a great castle, Father Brown is drawn into a mystery surrounding the castle's lonely inhabitant. As the story goes, the brokenhearted Marquis of Marne, Jim Mair, killed his own beloved cousin, Maurice, in a duel over a lady thirty years ago. He has been hiding out ever since, attended only (local gossip alleges) by his priest-confessors, who supposedly keep him isolated from the world. The group—which includes a young Catholic named Mallow, a newspaper proprietor by the name of Sir John Cockspur (who has a vendetta against priests), and the Marquis' old friends, General and Lady Outram—returns later with the lady in question to "storm the castle" and officially welcome Jim back into polite society. But instead they are greeted by Father Brown, who has learned the truth.]

The only figure that came out of the cavernous castle doorway was the short and shabby figure of Father Brown.

"Look here," he said, in his simple, bothered fashion. "I told you you'd much better leave him alone. He knows what he's doing and it'll only make everybody unhappy."

Lady Outram, who was accompanied by a tall and quietly-dressed lady, still very handsome, presumably the original Miss Grayson, looked at the little priest with cold contempt.

"Really, sir," she said; "this is a very private occasion, and I don't understand what you have to do with it."

"Trust a priest to have to do with a private occasion," snarled Sir John Cockspur. "Don't you know they live behind the scenes like rats behind a wainscot burrowing their way into everybody's private rooms. See how he's already in possession of poor Marne." Sir John was slightly sulky, as his aristocratic friends had persuaded him to give up the great scoop of publicity in return for the privilege of being really inside a Society secret. It never occurred to him to ask himself whether he was at all like a rat in a wainscot.

"Oh, that's all right," said Father Brown, with the impatience of anxiety. "I've talked it over with the marquis and the only priest he's ever had anything to do with; his clerical tastes have been much exaggerated. I tell you he knows what he's about; and I do implore you all to leave him alone."

"You mean to leave him to this living death of moping and going mad in a ruin!" cried Lady Outram, in a voice that shook a little. "And all because he had the bad luck to shoot a man in a duel more than a quarter of a century ago. Is that what you call Christian charity?"

"Yes," answered the priest stolidly; "that is what I call Christian charity."

"It's about all the Christian charity you'll ever get out of these priests," cried Cockspur bitterly. "That's their only idea of pardoning a poor fellow for a piece of folly; to wall him up alive and starve him to death with fasts and penances and pictures of hell-fire. And all because a bullet went wrong."

"Really, Father Brown," said General Outram, "do you honestly think he deserves this? Is that your Christianity?"

"Surely the true Christianity," pleaded his wife more gently, "is that which knows all and pardons all; the love that can remember — and forget."

"Father Brown," said young Mallow, very earnestly, "I generally agree with what you say; but I'm hanged if I can follow you here. A shot in a duel, followed instantly by remorse, is not such an awful offense."

"I admit," said Father Brown dully, "that I take a more serious view of his offense."

"God soften your hard heart," said the strange lady speaking for the first time. "I am going to speak to my old friend."

Almost as if her voice had raised a ghost in that great grey house, something stirred within and a figure stood in the dark doorway at the top of the great stone flight of steps. It was clad in dead black, but there was something wild about the blanched hair and something in the pale features that was like the wreck of a marble statue.

Viola Grayson began calmly to move up the great flight of steps. . . . The tall lady proudly mounted the last step and came face to face with the Marquis of Marne. His lips moved, but something happened before he could speak.

A scream rang across the open space and went wailing away in echoes along those hollow walls. By the abruptness and agony with which it broke from the woman's lips it might have been a mere inarticulate cry. But it was an articulated word; and they all heard it with a horrible distinctness.

"Maurice!"

"What is it, dear?" cried Lady Outram, and began to run up the steps; for the other woman was swaying as if she might fall down the whole stone flight. Then she faced about and began to descend, all bowed and shrunken and shuddering. "Oh, my God," she was saying. "Oh, my God, it isn't Jim at all. It's Maurice!"

"I think, Lady Outram," said the priest gravely, "you had better go with your friend."

As they turned, a voice fell on them like a stone from the top of the stone stair, a voice that might have come out of an open grave. It was hoarse and unnatural, like the voices of men who are left alone with wild birds on desert islands. It was the voice of the Marquis of Marne, and it said: "Stop!"

"Father Brown," he said, "before your friends disperse I authorize you to tell them all I have told you. Whatever follows, I will hide from it no longer."

"You are right," said the priest, "and it shall be counted to you.". . .

[Editor's note: Father Brown then explains what he has learned: It was not Maurice who was killed in the duel, but Jim. Through an elaborate deception, Maurice disappeared and has allowed his friends to believe the reverse all these years.]

. . . The rest of the company had risen and stood staring down at the narrator with pale faces. "Are you sure of this?" asked Sir John at last, in a thick voice.

"I am sure of it," said Father Brown, "and now I leave Maurice Mair, the present Marquis of Marne, to your Christian charity. You have told me something to-day about Christian charity. You seemed to me to give it almost too large a place; but how fortunate it is for poor sinners like this man that you err so much on the side of mercy, and are ready to be reconciled to all mankind."

"Hang it all," exploded the general; "if you think I'm going to be reconciled to a filthy viper like that, I tell you I wouldn't say a word to save him from hell. I said I could pardon a regular decent duel, but of all the treacherous assassins—" . . .

. . . "I wouldn't touch him with a barge-pole myself," said Mallow.

"There is a limit to human charity," said Lady Outram, trembling all over.

"There is," said Father Brown dryly; "and that is the real difference between human charity and Christian charity. You must forgive me if I was not altogether crushed by your contempt for my uncharitableness to-day; or by the lectures you read me about pardon for every sinner. For it seems to me that you only pardon the sins that you don't really think sinful. You only forgive criminals when they commit what you don't regard as crimes, but rather as conventions. So you tolerate a conventional duel, just as you tolerate a conventional divorce. You forgive because there isn't anything to be forgiven."

"But, hang it all," cried Mallow, "you don't expect us to be able to pardon a vile thing like this?"

"No," said the priest; "but *we* have to be able to pardon it."

He stood up abruptly and looked round at them.

"We have to touch such men, not with a bargepole, but with a benediction," he said. "We have to say the word that will save them from hell. We alone are left to deliver them from despair when your human charity deserts them. Go on your own primrose path pardoning all your favorite vices and being generous to your fashionable crimes; and leave us in the darkness, vampires of the night, to console those who really need consolation; who do things really indefensible, things that neither the world nor they themselves can defend; and none but a priest will pardon. Leave us with the men who commit the mean and revolting and real crimes; mean as St. Peter when the cock crew, and yet the dawn came."

"The dawn," repeated Mallow doubtfully. "You mean hope—for him?"

"Yes," replied the other. "Let me ask you one question. You are great ladies and men of honor and secure of yourselves; you would never, you can tell yourselves, stoop to such squalid reason as that. But tell me this. If any of you had so stooped, which of you, years afterwards, when you were old and rich and safe, would have been driven by conscience or confessor to tell such a story of yourself? You say you could not commit so base a crime. Could you confess so base a crime?"

The others gathered their possessions together and drifted by twos and threes out of the room in silence. And Father Brown, also in silence, went back to the melancholy castle of Marne.

# HOLY WEDNESDAY

## Willing to Suffer

### OPENING PRAYER

O my Lord and my all!
How canst thou wish us to prize
such a wretched existence?
We could not desist from longing
and begging thee to take us from it,
were it not for the hope of losing it
for thy sake or devoting it entirely to thy service
—and above all because we know
it is thy will that we should live.
—Teresa of Avila (Spanish, 1515–1582)

### SCRIPTURES

Psalm 70 | Isaiah 53:1–6 | Philippians 2:1–11 |
Mark 12:1–12; 14:32–42

### READINGS

"Truly no man can ransom another" by Katherine James
"The Stigmata of Francis" by Abigail Carroll
"Crucifying" by John Donne
"Christ in the Garden of Olives" by Richard Jones
"Elder Brother" by Susan McCaslin
"O Deus, ego amo te" by Gerard Manley Hopkins
From *The Light Princess* by George MacDonald

### PERSONAL PRAYER AND REFLECTION

### CLOSING PRAYER

Since it is so,
'Let us die with thee!'
as St. Thomas said,
for to be away from thee
is but to die again and again,
haunted as we are
by the dread of losing thee forever!
—TERESA OF AVILA (Spanish, 1515–1582)

## READINGS

### *Truly no man can ransom another*
KATHERINE JAMES (Anglo-American, contemporary)

Or give to God the price of his life[16]
If there is a kettle steaming
It is there for the battle inside
The structure that changes
From water to fog
And a mist rising damp to the ceiling

If a person seeks to have moments
And stretches during which
Molecules transgress
Their state and buzz unaware
In temperatures worth noting
Because of the changes within,
Then truly it is the heat that gives life
Not the ransom of another
Or replacement of structure

One life gives life that is life
If life came from that first
Boil, then reach for the heat
And plunge into the horror
Of molecule's rapid chant
Over and over

The love the love the love
Your love that ransoms me

———

## The Stigmata of Francis
ABIGAIL CARROLL (Anglo-American, contemporary)

After the nails, the hush
    of a seraph's wings as you lay
      on the grass in the hold of those luminous

arms—your eyes three-quarters
    closed, your head turned slightly
      back. In the distance, a smooth and lonely moon-

glossed pond. Caravaggio
    made a study of your hands,
      fingers curled in an open clutch around your

unseen wounds: the right
    just below a tear in your frock
      where the sword-tip pierced your side, the left

cupping a prayer, palm up—
    even as it dangles down in pain.
      Some say the love of God can cause a man

to faint, plow him down,
    drive him mad, take him
      wholly to the ground. That force that filled

the void with breath unhinged
  a Hebrew's hip, struck a Roman blind,
   but you had nothing left to lose that night the sky

called out your name—nothing
  to lose but yourself to the wild of a love
   the stars had never seen, the blazing hills could not

explain. Life held no claim
  on you now, the artist knew, so
   he rendered you half dead, laid out as Christ

in Mary's arms, only here
  a seraph holds your wilted frame,
   supports your tilted head above his angled knee.

His wings are close,
  the feathers soft and real.
   They ruffle in the late-night breeze.

———

## Crucifying
JOHN DONNE (English, 1572–1631)

*By miracles exceeding power of man,*
He faith in some, envy in some begat,
For, what weak spirits admire, ambitious hate;
In both affections many to him ran,
But Oh! the worst are most, they will and can,
Alas, and do, unto the immaculate,
Whose creature Fate is, now prescribe a fate,
Measuring self-life's infinity to a span,
Nay to an inch. Lo, where condemned he
Bears his own cross, with pain, yet by and by

When it bears him, he must bear more and die.
Now thou art lifted up, draw me to thee,
And at thy death giving such liberal dole,
*Moist, with one drop of thy blood, my dry soul.*

———

## Christ in the Garden of Olives
RICHARD JONES (Anglo-American, contemporary)

*Church of Saint-Paul-Saint-Louis*

Only steps from the apartment,
I steal down the alley
and through the red side doors of the church
to meditate once more on Delacroix's altarpiece.

My wooden chair leans back against a stone column.
Under the crossing's high dome,
candles flicker like stars through the olive trees.
Lord, how many days have I come here

to be with your sleeping disciples
and the three angels hovering in the darkness?
And why did it take me so long to see
you are not waiting for the soldiers

with their torches and weapons to arrest you,
not waiting for Pilate to condemn you?
Already you are lifting your arms
to the executioner's hammer and nails.

———

## Elder Brother
Susan McCaslin (Canadian, contemporary)

Jesus, who could bear to be you,
carving out centuries with your metaphors—

buried pearls, cryptic, enigmatic tales,
your ragtag band of fishermen and thieves.

Little you care whether we remember you
as human or God. All that prickly disputation.

Your kingdom is still a child,
something lost and found.

Non-violent, yet such a guerrilla
you got yourself killed,

knew what that flattening death meant,
a showdown on a field, a sign.

To live like a field lily, springing back—
a few have done it.

———

## O Deus, ego amo te[17]
Gerard Manley Hopkins (English, 1844–1889)

O God, I love thee, I love thee—
Not out of hope of heaven for me
Nor fearing not to love and be
    In the everlasting burning.
Thou, thou, my Jesus, after me
    Didst reach thine arms out dying,
For my sake sufferedst nails and lance
Mocked and marréd countenance,

Sorrows passing number,
Sweat and care and cumber,
Yea and death, and this for me,
And thou couldst see me sinning:
Then I, why should not I love thee,
Jesu so much in love with me?
Not for heaven's sake; not to be
Out of hell by loving thee;
Not for any gains I see;
But just the way that thou didst me
I do love and I will love thee:
What must I love thee, Lord, for then?—
For being my king and God. Amen.

———

## From *The Light Princess*
### George MacDonald (Scottish, 1824–1905)

[Editor's note: In MacDonald's fairytale, a princess is born without gravity (hence, *light*): not only does she float, but she seems unable to practice empathy or understand how her actions affect others. When the nearby lake mysteriously begins to drain and it becomes clear that her life and flourishing diminish in proportion, a prince whom she has met before (disguised as a servant) volunteers to plug the hole in the bottom of the lake with his own body. This, of course, means that as the lake rises, he will surely die. Meanwhile, the king has agreed to the prince's only concession, that the princess keep him company in a nearby boat.]

The prince went to dress for the occasion, for he was resolved to die like a prince.

When the princess heard that a man had offered to die for her, she was so transported that she jumped off the bed, feeble as she was, and danced about the room for joy. She did not care who the man was; that was nothing to her. The hole wanted stopping; and if only a man would do, why, take one. In an hour or two more everything was ready. Her maid dressed her in haste, and they carried her to the side of the lake. When she saw it she shrieked, and covered her face with her hands. They bore her across to the stone where they had already placed a little boat for her.

The water was not deep enough to float it, but they hoped it would be, before long. They laid her on cushions, placed in the boat wines and fruits and other nice things, and stretched a canopy over all.

In a few minutes the prince appeared. The princess recognized him at once, but did not think it worth while to acknowledge him.

"Here I am," said the prince. "Put me in."

"They told me it was a shoeblack," said the princess.

"So I am," said the prince. "I blacked your little boots three times a day, because they were all I could get of you. Put me in."

The courtiers did not resent his bluntness, except by saying to each other that he was taking it out in impudence.

But how was he to be put in? The golden plate contained no instructions on this point. The prince looked at the hole, and saw but one way. He put both his legs into it, sitting on the stone, and, stooping forward, covered the corner that remained open with his two hands. In this uncomfortable position he resolved to abide his fate, and turning to the people, said,—

"Now you can go."

The king had already gone home to dinner.

"Now you can go," repeated the princess after him, like a parrot.

The people obeyed her and went.

Presently a little wave flowed over the stone, and wetted one of the prince's knees. But he did not mind it much. He began to sing, and the song he sang was this:—

*"As a world that has no well,*
*Darting bright in forest dell;*
*As a world without the gleam*
*Of the downward-going stream;*
*As a world without the glance*
*Of the ocean's fair expanse;*
*As a world where never rain*
*Glittered on the sunny plain;—*
*Such, my heart, thy world would be,*
*If no love did flow in thee.*

*As a world without the sound*
*Of the rivulets underground;*
*Or the bubbling of the spring*
*Out of darkness wandering;*
*Or the mighty rush and flowing*
*Of the river's downward going;*
*Or the music-showers that drop*
*On the outspread beech's top;*
*Or the ocean's mighty voice,*
*When his lifted waves rejoice;—*
*Such, my soul, thy world would be,*
*If no love did sing in thee.*

*Lady, keep thy world's delight;*
*Keep the waters in thy sight.*
*Love hath made me strong to go,*
*For thy sake, to realms below,*
*Where the water's shine and hum*
*Through the darkness never come;*
*Let, I pray, one thought of me*
*Spring, a little well, in thee;*
*Lest thy loveless soul be found*
*Like a dry and thirsty ground."*

"Sing again, prince. It makes it less tedious," said the princess.

But the prince was too much overcome to sing any more, and a long pause followed.

"This is very kind of you, prince," said the princess at last, quite coolly, as she lay in the boat with her eyes shut.

"I am sorry I can't return the compliment," thought the prince; "but you are worth dying for, after all."

Again a wavelet, and another, and another flowed over the stone, and wetted both the prince's knees; but he did not speak or move. Two—three—four hours passed in this way, the princess apparently asleep, and the prince very patient. But he was much disappointed in his position, for he had none of the consolation he had hoped for.

At last he could bear it no longer.

"Princess!" said he.

But at the moment up started the princess, crying,—

"I'm afloat! I'm afloat!"

And the little boat bumped against the stone.

"Princess!" repeated the prince, encouraged by seeing her wide awake and looking eagerly at the water.

"Well?" said she, without looking round.

"Your papa promised that you should look at me, and you haven't looked at me once."

"Did he? Then I suppose I must. But I am so sleepy!"

"Sleep then, darling, and don't mind me," said the poor prince.

"Really, you are very good," replied the princess. "I think I will go to sleep again."

"Just give me a glass of wine and a biscuit first," said the prince, very humbly.

"With all my heart," said the princess, and gaped as she said it.

She got the wine and the biscuit, however, and leaning over the side of the boat towards him, was compelled to look at him.

"Why, prince," she said, "you don't look well! Are you sure you don't mind it?"

"Not a bit," answered he, feeling very faint indeed. "Only I shall die before it is of any use to you, unless I have something to eat."

"There, then," said she, holding out the wine to him.

"Ah! you must feed me. I dare not move my hands. The water would run away directly."

"Good gracious!" said the princess; and she began at once to feed him with bits of biscuit and sips of wine.

As she fed him, he contrived to kiss the tips of her fingers now and then. She did not seem to mind it, one way or the other. But the prince felt better.

"Now for your own sake, princess," said he, "I cannot let you go to sleep. You must sit and look at me, else I shall not be able to keep up."

"Well, I will do anything I can to oblige you," answered she, with condescension; and, sitting down, she did look at him, and kept looking at him with wonderful steadiness, considering all things.

The sun went down, and the moon rose, and, gush after gush, the waters were rising up the prince's body. They were up to his waist now.

"Why can't we go and have a swim?" said the princess. "There seems to be water enough just about here."

"I shall never swim more," said the prince.

"Oh, I forgot," said the princess, and was silent.

So the water grew and grew, and rose up and up on the prince. And the princess sat and looked at him. She fed him now and then. The night wore on. The waters rose and rose. The moon rose likewise higher and higher, and shone full on the face of the dying prince. The water was up to his neck.

"Will you kiss me, princess?" said he, feebly.

The nonchalance was all gone now.

"Yes, I will," answered the princess, and kissed him with a long, sweet, cold kiss.

"Now," said he, with a sigh of content, "I die happy."

He did not speak again. The princess gave him some wine for the last time: he was past eating. Then she sat down again, and looked at him. The water rose and rose. It touched his chin. It touched his lower lip. It touched between his lips. He shut them hard to keep it out. The princess began to feel strange. It touched his upper lip. He breathed through his nostrils. The princess looked wild. It covered his nostrils. Her eyes looked scared, and shone strange in the moonlight. His head fell back; the water closed over it, and the bubbles of his last breath bubbled up through the water.

# MAUNDY THURSDAY

## *The Accused*

OPENING PRAYER

No! I have ran the way of wickedness,
Forgetting what my faith should follow most;
I did not think upon thy holiness,
Nor by my sins what sweetness I have lost.
Oh sin! for sin hath compassed me about,
That, Lord, I know not where to find thee out.
—MARY HERBERT, COUNTESS OF PEMBROKE (English, 1561–1621)

SCRIPTURES

PSALM 35 | ISAIAH 53:7–12 | REVELATION 18:21–24 | MARK 14:53–72

READINGS

"Byzantine Gold" by DERRICK AUSTIN
"Thursday" by HANNAH FAITH NOTESS
"Inertia" by JILL PELÁEZ BAUMGAERTNER
"A Witness to Process" by ANNA KAMIEŃSKA
"The Revolutionary" by LUCI SHAW
From *The Brothers Karamazov* by FYODOR DOSTOEVSKY

PERSONAL PRAYER AND REFLECTION

CLOSING PRAYER

O help, my God! Let not their plot
   Kill them and me,
   And also thee,

Who art my life: dissolve the knot,
As the sun scatters by his light
All the rebellions of the night.
—GEORGE HERBERT (English, 1593–1633)


## READINGS


## Byzantine Gold
DERRICK AUSTIN (African-American, contemporary)

A chain of blue-white chips mimics waves
       pleating
   around Christ's body. On the western wall,

another scene of owl-eyed saints
       drawing light
   unlike us. Despite centuries of votive smoke,

the shining ranks of prophets gesture,
       elegant
   as sommeliers, toward mosaic scrolls

and would have you consider the honeycombed
       geometry
   of paradise—dome, arch, and column—

it's nearly perfect with its air of permanence,
       above penitent
   and tourist, above the fray

of ethnic cleansing it would have us believe:
       a Balkan
   landmine planted near trillium,

the scarred field, the ghost limbs of olive trees,
    and the boy
  there, I mean, he's a man now,

about my age, passing us on his prosthetic leg—
    that which was
  sundered brilliantly shining—though

he might have been a child when he lost the limb.
    Think invention.
  Think miracle. To think someone, Doctors

Without Borders, maybe, could make a man whole again.
    But look:
  a mortar leveled Gethsemane,

a Visigoth defaced the deposition, and,
    her turquoise
  hem unraveling, poor Mary's going to pieces,

pocked by shrapnel from a mislaid bomb.
    If the dome
  cracked open, what a dry comb it would be.

We consider paradise anew despite its stone
    indifference
  to time. Christ Pantocrator, alien, severe,

claims the apse, suspended in gold
    leaf, apart
  from and a part of the world, the dust

those semiprecious stones become. We would find
    comfort
  in his Renaissance flesh,

its bordello-shades of pain—the oils
    of the canvas
  like the oils of the body—but where

would we find warmth beneath these glass eyes,
    radiant,
      petrifying? His gaze arrests us

like everything we make, which is touched
    with our image:
      metals and mirroring glass

in mortal shapes, even the minefield,
    visionary
      in its violence—God before Sodom

would be amazed by such force. The mind
    itself
      drips rough honey and gilds the world.

————

## Thursday
HANNAH FAITH NOTESS (Anglo-American, contemporary)

Hands harvested the grapes, and feet crushed
them in the winepress. Hands held
the vessel under the dark stream
till the vessel ran over, sealed up the wine
and carried it down to the cellar.

Hands shaped the water basin on the wheel,
set it to dry. Hands worked the loom that wove
the towel now folded under the basin.
Fingers held the needle that, hemming
the towel's edge, drew a drop of blood.

Hands kneaded the unleavened dough,
worked in more flour, stoked the oven coals.

Hands shaped the loaves and baked them,
then set the bread to cool.

Hands picked and washed the bitter herbs.
Hands laid the table, lit the lamps.

And when supper ends and hands raise up
the cup, the men will remember (though
nobody will say), the hands that drew the knife
across the lamb's throat and held its limbs
while the last twitch of muscle ebbed away.

———

## Inertia

JILL PELÁEZ BAUMGAERTNER (Cuban-American, contemporary)

### I.

Somewhere someone is hammering,
a caged dove coos,
her flight rattle silenced. Pilate

stands, one hand on his hip,
his palms sticky, fresh from
morning plums, so ripe

the juice as it trickled down his throat,
as he bit into flesh
as dark as his mouth.

### II.

*Are you the King of the
Jews?* he asks,
and before the last word leaves

Pilate's mouth, the other
one says, *You say so,*
*Jew* and *You*

blending into the answer
latent in the seamless
interrogative.

### III.

The others yell their threats,
their old fears, their questions
of both. They are a garble of anger.

Then Pilate once again:
*Listen: Do you not hear their*
*complaints?* Jesus is not resigned.

This is the quiet of termites.
It is the silence of the vein of silver
underneath the mountain's

grimace, helpless to resist the mud's
cracked reclumping, the boulders'
stance nudged into acceleration,

the ground once steady and dependable
now curling under the earth's crust
rumbling under its elastic waves.

————

## A Witness to Process
ANNA KAMIEŃSKA (Polish, 1920–1986)

All out of breath he was telling it
as if he had just come back from the courts

that He stood so serene and upright
denied nothing
and was silent when jostled
and didn't respond to the words
What is truth
but everyone could see it was He who is the truth

So He was found innocent No
guilty
So all were on His side No
against Him
So He was imprisoned No
hanged
So no one protested No
one denied

———

## The Revolutionary
LUCI SHAW (naturalized U.S. citizen, contemporary)

Do you wince when
you hear his name
made vanity?

What if you were not so safe,
sheltered, circled by love
and tradition? What if
the world shouted at you?
Could you take the string of
hoarse words—glutton, wino,
devil, crazy man, agitator, bastard,
nigger-lover, rebel—
and hang the grimy ornament

around your neck
and answer *love?*

See the sharp stones poised
against your head! Even
your dear friend
couples your name with curses
("By God, I know not God!").
The obscene affirmation
of infidelity
echoes, insistent,
from a henhouse roof.

Then, Slap! Spit! The whip,
the thorn. The gravel
grinds your fallen knees
under a whole world's weight
until the hammering home
of all your virtue
stakes you, stranded,
halfway between hilltop
and heaven (neither will
have you).

And will you whisper
*forgive?*

———

FROM *The Brothers Karamazov*
FYODOR DOSTOEVSKY (Russian, 1821–1881)

[Editor's note: In one of the most famous passages in all literature,
the most intellectual of the brothers Karamazov, Ivan, shares with
his pious younger brother, Alyosha, a *poeima* he has invented. It's a

scenario in which Jesus returns to earth during the Spanish Inquisition and is arrested and thrown into prison. There he is visited by the Cardinal Grand Inquisitor of the Ecclesiastical Court, who lays out a lengthy argument for why he believes Jesus failed the three temptations by Satan (see Luke 4:1–13) and should be executed—again. Below is just a snippet of the monologue.]

In the pitch darkness the iron door of the prison is suddenly opened and the Grand Inquisitor himself comes in with a light in his hand. He is alone; the door is closed at once behind him. He stands in the doorway and for a minute or two gazes into His face. At last he goes up slowly, sets the light on the table, and speaks.

"Is it you? You?" But receiving no answer, he adds at once, "Don't answer, be silent. What can you say, indeed? I know too well what you would say. And you have no right to add anything to what you said of old. Why, then, are you come to hinder us? For you have come to hinder us, and you know it. But do you know what will happen tomorrow? I don't know who you are and don't care to know whether it is you or only a semblance of Him, but tomorrow I shall condemn you and burn you at the stake as the worst of heretics. And the very people who have today kissed your feet, tomorrow at the faintest sign from me will rush to heap up the embers of your fire. Do you know that? Yes, maybe you know it," he added with thoughtful penetration, never for a moment taking his eyes off the Prisoner. . . .

". . . There are three powers, three powers alone, able to conquer and to hold captive forever the conscience of these impotent rebels for their happiness—those forces are miracle, mystery, and authority. You have rejected all three and have set the example for doing so. When the wise and dread spirit set you on the pinnacle of the temple and said to you, 'If you would know whether you are the Son of God then cast yourself down, for it is written: the angels shall hold him up lest he fall and bruise himself, and you shall know then whether you are the Son of God and shall prove then how great is your faith in your Father.' But you did refuse and wouldn't cast yourself down. Oh, of course, you did so proudly and well, like God; but the weak, unruly race of men, are they gods? Oh, you knew then that in taking one step, in making one movement to cast yourself down, you would be tempting God and lost all your faith in him, and would have been dashed to pieces against that earth which you came to save. And the wise spirit that tempted you would have rejoiced. But I ask again, are there many like you? And could you believe for one moment that men, too, could face such a temptation? Is the nature of men such, that they can reject miracle, and at the great moments of their life, the moments of their deepest, most agonizing spiritual difficulties, cling only to the free verdict of the heart? Oh, you knew that your deed would be recorded in books, would be handed down to remote times and the utmost ends of the earth, and you hoped that man, following you, would cling to God and not ask for a miracle. But you didn't know that when man rejects miracle he rejects God too; for man seeks not so much God as the miraculous. And as man cannot bear to be without the miraculous, he will create new miracles of his own for himself, and will worship deeds of sorcery and witchcraft, though he might be a hundred times over a rebel, heretic, and infidel. You didn't come down from the Cross when they shouted to you, mocking and reviling you, 'Come down from the cross and we will believe that you are He.' You didn't come down, for again you wouldn't enslave man by a miracle, and you craved faith given freely, not based on miracle. You craved free love and not the base raptures of the slave before the might that has overawed him for ever. But you thought too highly of men therein, for they are slaves, of course, though rebellious by nature. Look round and judge; fifteen centuries have passed, look upon them. Whom have you raised up to yourself? I swear, man is weaker and baser by nature than you have believed him! Can he, can he do what you did? By showing him so much respect, you did, as it were, cease to feel for him, for you asked far too much from him—you who have loved him more than yourself! Respecting him less, you would have asked less of him. That would have been more like love, for his burden would have been lighter. He is weak and vile. So what if now he is everywhere rebelling against our power, and proud of his rebellion? It is the pride of a child and a schoolboy. They are little children rioting and barring out the teacher at school. But their childish delight will end; it will cost them dear. They will cast down temples and drench the earth with blood. But they will see at last, the foolish children, that, though they are rebels, they are impotent rebels, unable to keep up their own rebellion. Bathed in their foolish tears, they will recognize at last that He who created them rebels must have meant to mock at them. They will say this in despair, and their utterance will be a blasphemy which will make them more unhappy still, for man's nature cannot bear blasphemy, and in the end always avenges it on itself. And so unrest, confusion and unhappiness—that is the present lot of man after you bore so much for their freedom! The great prophet tells in vision and in image, that he saw all those who took part in the first resurrection and that there were of each tribe twelve thousand. But if there were so many of them, they must have been not men but gods. They had borne your cross, they had endured scores of years in the barren, hungry wilderness, living upon locusts and roots—and you may indeed point with pride at those children of freedom, of free love, of free and splendid sacrifice for your name. But remember that they were only some thousands; and what of the rest? And how are the other weak ones to blame, because they could not endure what the strong have endured? How is the weak soul to blame that it is unable to receive such terrible gifts? Can you have simply come to the elect and for the elect? But if so, it is a mystery and we cannot understand it. And if it is a mystery, we too have a right to preach a mystery, and to teach them that it's not the free judgment of their hearts, not love that matters, but a mystery which they must follow blindly, even against their conscience. So we have done. We have corrected your work and have founded it upon *miracle, mystery* and *authority*. And men rejoiced that they were again led like sheep, and that the terrible gift that had brought them such suffering was, at last, lifted from their hearts. Were we right teaching them this? Speak! Did we not love mankind, so meekly acknowledging their feebleness, lovingly lightening their burden, and permitting their weak nature even sin with our sanction? Why have you come now to hinder us? And why do you look silently and searchingly at me with your mild eyes? Be angry. I don't want your love, for I love you not. And what use is it for me to hide anything from you? Don't I know to Whom I am speaking? All that I can say is known to you already. And is it for me to conceal from you our mystery? Perhaps it is your will to hear it from my lips. Listen, then. We are not working with you, but with *him*—that is our mystery. It's long—eight centuries—since we have been on *his* side and not on yours. Just eight centuries ago, we took from him what you rejected with scorn, that last gift he offered you, showing you all the kingdoms of the earth. We took from him Rome and the sword of Cæsar, and proclaimed ourselves sole rulers of the earth, though hitherto we have not been able to complete our work. But whose fault is that? Oh, the work is only beginning, but it has begun. . . ."

## GOOD FRIDAY

*The Spent Word*

OPENING PRAYER

. . . For me in tortures thou resignest thy breath,
Embraced me on the cross, and saved me by death.
And can these sufferings fail my heart to move?
Such as then was, and is, thy love to me,
Such, and shall be still, my love to thee—
To thee, Redeemer! mercy's sacred spring!
My God, my Father, Maker, and my King!
—ALEXANDER POPE (English, 1688–1744)

SCRIPTURES

PSALM 22 | ISAIAH 52:7–15 | ROMANS 5:1–11 | MARK 15:1–39

READINGS

"Good Friday" by GEORGE HERBERT
"Bell" by JEANNE MURRAY WALKER
"The Face" by RICHARD JONES
"Friday" by HANNAH FAITH NOTESS
"Instructions to an Artisan" by AMIT MAJMUDAR
From "The Dream of the Rood," AUTHOR UNKNOWN
From *A Tale of Two Cities* by CHARLES DICKENS

PERSONAL PRAYER AND REFLECTION

CLOSING PRAYER

You Who shattered the fire of the flaming sword,
Who gathered to paradise—for the sake of his plea

for pity—the thief crucified by Your side,
remember me also in Your kingdom.
I too have been crucified with You.
For fear of You, I have nailed down my flesh,
trembling as I await your judgments.
—MACRINA THE YOUNGER (Turkish, ca. 327–379)
adapted by Scott Cairns

# READINGS

## Good Friday
GEORGE HERBERT (English, 1593–1633)

### I.

O my chief good,
How shall I measure out thy blood?
How shall I count what thee befell,
    And each grief tell?

Shall I thy woes
Number according to thy foes?
Or, since one star show'd thy first breath,
    Shall all thy death?

Or shall each leaf,
Which falls in Autumn, score a grief?
Or cannot leaves, but fruit, be sign,
    Of the true vine?

Then let each hour
Of my whole life one grief devour;
That thy distress through all may run,
    And be my sun.

> Or rather let
> My several sins their sorrows get;
> That, as each beast his cure doth know,
> >  Each sin may so.

> #### II.
> Since blood is fittest, Lord, to write
> Thy sorrows in, and bloody fight;
> My heart hath store; write there, where in
> One box doth lie both ink and sin:

> That when Sin spies so many foes,
> Thy whips, thy nails, thy wounds, thy woes,
> All come to lodge there, Sin may say,
> *No room for me,* and fly away.

> Sin being gone, O fill the place,
> And keep possession with thy grace;
> Lest sin take courage and return,
> And all the writings blot or burn.

---

## Bell

Jeanne Murray Walker (Anglo-American, contemporary)

— *Good Friday, 2004*

Since time flies one way like an arrow,
the sugar can't be stirred out of your oatmeal,
and no matter how long the murderer sobs
on the median strip—*sorry!*—she can't reverse
her swerve, cannot rescind her drink

before the crash. Was Jesus heartsick
to find history is not a zipper running both ways?
He who loved eternity—its roominess,
its reversibility—did he have to learn
as he grew up that he never could unsay a thing,

once said? And yet today, like all Good Fridays,
He hangs on the cross again. On altars
he hangs. On necklaces. His death is like an x
that rides the wheel of time, showing up again
in ritual, that miniature eternity, that spring

re-sprung. Dear God, there in your big eternity,
remember that your hands and feet can never
be unscarred again. Hear these words spoken
by a body that suffers, by a tongue
that will stiffen and be gone.

Have mercy on us who love time.
May this prayer be a tire that rolls
over every inch of whatever way
to find You. May it be a bell
which can never be unrung.

———

## The Face
RICHARD JONES (Anglo-American, contemporary)

> *Emmet Till's mother*
> *speaking over the radio*

She tells in a comforting voice
what it was like to touch her dead boy's face,

how she'd lingered and traced
the broken jaw, the crushed eyes—

the face *that* badly beaten, disfigured—
before confirming his identity.

And then she compares his face to
the face of Jesus, dying on the cross.

This mother says no, she'd not recognize
her Lord, for he was beaten far, far worse

than the son she loved with all her heart.
For, she said, she could still discern her son's curved earlobe,

but the face of Christ
was beaten to death by the whole world.

———

## Friday

HANNAH FAITH NOTESS (Anglo-American, contemporary)

Maybe the prisoner's mother
didn't block her ears against
the swinging whip, the dragging
chain, the buzz of voltage
that set off fireworks in the brain.
Maybe she has strength to hold

his body one more time, once
it is finished. And maybe the body
is a darkness into which we must
keep looking. But there is more
pain already on this earth
than most of us can bear.

Why should we look
upon the same splayed form
so often that we notice only

how bony his knees are
in one painting, how taut
the skin of his pierced side

in another? Take him down
and let his mother hold him.
Let him be buried, let
the story's pages turn. And when
the earth splits, when the veil
is torn, when the dead stumble

dazed from the tombs, trailing
their moldy bandages behind them,
let the thunderclap announce
that agony flows only outward
from broken blood vessels,
no longer settling in the soul.

———

## Instructions to an Artisan

Amit Majmudar (Indian-American, contemporary)

Into the rood wood, where the grain's current splits
around the stones of its knots, carve eyelashes and eyelids.
Dye the knots, too—indigo, ink-black, vermillion
irises. These will be his eyes, always open, willing
themselves not to close when dust rises or sweat falls,
eyes witnessing, dimly, the eclipse that shawls
the shuddering hill, Jerusalem's naked shoulder.
The body itself? From a wick that still whiffs of smolder,
wax, because wax sloughs a smooth skein on the fingers just
below sensation's threshold. Prop the cross
upright and let the tear-hot wax trickle, slow, clot, taper
into a torso, thighs, calves, feet. Of Gideon Bible paper,

thinner than skin, cut him his scrap of cloth; embed
iron shavings in his forehead,
and, as the wax cools, scrape the rust off an old fuel can
to salt the whole wound that is the man.
Cry, if you feel like crying, and if no one else is there.
Then set it on the counter with your other wares.

———

FROM *"The Dream of the Rood"*
UNKNOWN (Anglo-Saxon, ca. 750)

Lo! choicest of dreams I will relate,
What dream I dreamt in middle of night
When mortal men reposed in rest.
Methought I saw a wondrous wood
Tower aloft with light bewound,
Brightest of trees; that beacon was all
Begirt with gold; jewels were standing
Four at surface of earth, likewise were there five
Above on the shoulder-brace. All angels of God beheld it,
Fair through future ages; 'twas no criminal's cross indeed,
But holy spirits beheld it there,
Men upon earth, all this glorious creation.
Strange was that victor-tree, and stained with sins was I,
With foulness defiled. I saw the glorious tree
With vesture adorned winsomely shine,
Begirt with gold; bright gems had there
Worthily decked the tree of the Lord.
Yet through that gold I might perceive
Old strife of the wretched, that first it gave
Blood on the stronger side. With sorrows was I oppressed,
Afraid for that fair sight; I saw the ready beacon

Change in vesture and hue; at times with moisture covered,
Soiled with course of blood; at times with treasure adorned.
Yet lying there a longer while,
Beheld I sad the Savior's tree
Until I heard that words it uttered;
The best of woods gan[18] speak these words:
"'Twas long ago (I remember it still)
That I was hewn at the end of a grove,
Stripped from off my stem; strong foes laid hold of me there,
Wrought for themselves a show, bade felons raise me up;
Men bore me on their shoulders, till on a mount they set me;
Fiends many fixed me there. Then saw I mankind's Lord
Hasten with mickle[19] might, for He would sty[20] upon me.
There durst I not 'gainst word of the Lord
Bow down or break, when saw I tremble
The surface of earth; I might then all
My foes have felled, yet fast I stood.
The Hero young begirt Himself, Almighty God was He,
Strong and stern of mind; He stied on the gallows high,
Bold in sight of many, for man He would redeem.
I shook when the Hero clasped me, yet durst not bow to earth,
Fall to surface of earth, but firm I must there stand.
A rood was I upreared; I raised the mighty King
The Lord of Heaven; I durst not bend me.
They drove their dark nails through me; the wounds are seen upon me,
The open gashes of guile; I durst harm none of them.
They mocked us both together; all moistened with blood was I,
Shed from side of the man, when forth He sent His spirit.
Many have I on that mount endured
Of cruel fates; I saw the Lord of Hosts
Strongly outstretched; darkness had then
Covered with clouds the corse[21] of the Lord,
The brilliant brightness; the shadow continued,

Wan 'neath the welkin.[22] There wept all creation,
Bewailed the King's death; Christ was on the cross.
Yet hastening thither they came from afar
To the Son of the King: that all I beheld.
Sorely with sorrows was I oppressed; yet I bowed 'neath the hands
   of men,
Lowly with mickle might. Took they there Almighty God,
Him raised from the heavy torture; the battle-warriors left me
To stand bedrenched with blood; all wounded with darts was I.
There laid they the weary of limb, at head of His corse they stood,
Beheld the Lord of Heaven, and He rested Him there awhile,
Worn from the mickle war. Began they an earth-house to work,
Men in the murderers' sight, carved it of brightest stone,
Placed therein victory's Lord. Began sad songs to sing
The wretched at eventide; then would they back return
Mourning from the mighty prince; all lonely rested He there.
Yet weeping we then a longer while
Stood at our station: the voice arose
Of battle-warriors; the corse grew cold,
Fair house of life. Then one gan fell
Us all to earth; 'twas a fearful fate!
One buried us in deep pit, yet of me the thanes[23] of the Lord,
His friends, heard tell; [from earth they raised me],
And me begirt with gold and silver.
Now thou mayst hear, my dearest man,
That bale of woes have I endured,
Of sorrows sore. Now the time is come,
That me shall honor both far and wide
Men upon earth, and all this mighty creation
Will pray to this beacon. On me God's Son
Suffered awhile; so glorious now
I tower to Heaven, and I may heal
Each one of those who reverence me. . . ."

FROM *A Tale of Two Cities*
CHARLES DICKENS (English, 1812–1870)

[Editor's note: Eventually Charles Darnay (Evremonde) is tried again by the blood-thirsty court of the new French Republic and sentenced to death. But just before his scheduled execution, a friend by the name of Sydney Carton—who from their first encounter back in London could be his twin in appearance but polar opposite in character—manages to drug him and take his place. We find Carton now with a crowd of others in a holding room of the Bastille, all awaiting the Guillotine.]

As he stood by the wall in a dim corner, while some of the fifty-two were brought in after him, one man stopped in passing, to embrace him, as having a knowledge of him. It thrilled him with a great dread of discovery; but the man went on. A very few moments after that, a young woman, with a slight girlish form, a sweet spare face in which there was no vestige of color, and large widely opened patient eyes, rose from the seat where he had observed her sitting, and came to speak to him.

"Citizen Evremonde," she said, touching him with her cold hand. "I am a poor little seamstress, who was with you in La Force."

He murmured for answer: "True. I forget what you were accused of?"

"Plots. Though the just Heaven knows that I am innocent of any. Is it likely? Who would think of plotting with a poor little weak creature like me?"

The forlorn smile with which she said it, so touched him, that tears started from his eyes.

"I am not afraid to die, Citizen Evremonde, but I have done nothing. I am not unwilling to die, if the Republic which is to do so much good to us poor, will profit by my death; but I do not know how that can be, Citizen Evremonde. Such a poor weak little creature!"

As the last thing on earth that his heart was to warm and soften to, it warmed and softened to this pitiable girl.

"I heard you were released, Citizen Evremonde. I hoped it was true?"

"It was. But, I was again taken and condemned."

"If I may ride with you, Citizen Evremonde, will you let me hold your hand? I am not afraid, but I am little and weak, and it will give me more courage."

As the patient eyes were lifted to his face, he saw a sudden doubt in them, and then astonishment. He pressed the work-worn, hunger-worn young fingers, and touched his lips.

"Are you dying for him?" she whispered.

"And his wife and child. Hush! Yes."

"O you will let me hold your brave hand, stranger?"

"Hush! Yes, my poor sister; to the last." . . .

[Editor's Note: Carton, the young woman, and the others are piled onto carts, or tumbrils, and taken to the execution area.]

. . The tumbrils begin to discharge their loads. The ministers of Sainte Guillotine are robed and ready. Crash!—A head is held up, and the knitting-women who scarcely lifted their eyes to look at it a moment ago when it could think and speak, count One.

The second tumbril empties and moves on; the third comes up. Crash!—And the knitting-women, never faltering or pausing in their Work, count Two.

The supposed Evremonde descends, and the seamstress is lifted out next after him. He has not relinquished her patient hand in getting out, but still holds it as he promised. He gently places her with her back to the crashing engine that constantly whirrs up and falls, and she looks into his face and thanks him.

"But for you, dear stranger, I should not be so composed, for I am naturally a poor little thing, faint of heart; nor should I have been able to raise my thoughts to Him who was put to death, that we might have hope and comfort here to-day. I think you were sent to me by Heaven."

"Or you to me," says Sydney Carton. "Keep your eyes upon me, dear child, and mind no other object."

"I mind nothing while I hold your hand. I shall mind nothing when I let it go, if they are rapid."

"They will be rapid. Fear not!"

The two stand in the fast-thinning throng of victims, but they speak as if they were alone. Eye to eye, voice to voice, hand to hand, heart to heart, these two children of the Universal Mother, else so wide apart and differing, have come together on the dark highway, to repair home together, and to rest in her bosom.

"Brave and generous friend, will you let me ask you one last question? I am very ignorant, and it troubles me—just a little."

"Tell me what it is."

"I have a cousin, an only relative and an orphan, like myself, whom I love very dearly. She is five years younger than I, and she lives in a farmer's house in the south country. Poverty parted us, and she knows nothing of my fate—for I cannot write—and if I could, how should I tell her! It is better as it is."

"Yes, yes: better as it is."

"What I have been thinking as we came along, and what I am still thinking now, as I look into your kind strong face which gives me so much support, is this:—If the Republic really does good to the poor, and they come to be less hungry, and in all ways to suffer less, she may live a long time: she may even live to be old."

"What then, my gentle sister?"

"Do you think:" the uncomplaining eyes in which there is so much endurance, fill with tears, and the lips part a little more and tremble: "that it will seem long to me, while I wait for her in the better land where I trust both you and I will be mercifully sheltered?"

"It cannot be, my child; there is no Time there, and no trouble there."

"You comfort me so much! I am so ignorant. Am I to kiss you now? Is the moment come?"

"Yes."

She kisses his lips; he kisses hers; they solemnly bless each other. The spare hand does not tremble as he releases it; nothing worse than a sweet, bright constancy is in the patient face. She goes next before him—is gone; the knitting-women count Twenty-Two.

"I am the Resurrection and the Life, saith the Lord: he that believeth in me, though he were dead, yet shall he live: and whosoever liveth and believeth in me shall never die."

The murmuring of many voices, the upturning of many faces, the pressing on of many footsteps in the outskirts of the crowd, so that it swells forward in a mass, like one great heave of water, all flashes away. Twenty-Three.

# HOLY SATURDAY

## Between Midnight and Dawn

### OPENING PRAYER

O blessed body! Whither art thou thrown?
No lodging for thee, but a cold, hard stone?
So many hearts on earth, and yet not one
                                    Receive thee?
—GEORGE HERBERT (English, 1593–1633)

### SCRIPTURES

PSALM 25 | JOB 14:1–14 | ROMANS 5:12–21 | MATTHEW 27:57–66

### READINGS

"saturday." by AMEY VICTORIA ADKINS
"Bread turned to stone: Pietà" by LUCI SHAW
"Waiting to Be Filled" by EMILY GIBSON
"Easter Vigil" by JILL PELÁEZ BAUMGAERTNER
"Resurrection, imperfect" by JOHN DONNE
From *Can You See Anything Now* by KATHERINE JAMES

### PERSONAL PRAYER AND REFLECTION

### CLOSING PRAYER

Away, my life! Lord Christ, I have thy death:
My life's thy death, and thy death gives me breath.
But come, my life, I'll hide thee in his tomb:
The third day hence is not so long to come.
—RICHARD CRASHAW (English, 1612–1649)

*saturday.*

AMEY VICTORIA ADKINS (African-American, contemporary)

I grew where the blue of the mountains is so beautiful
you think you've drowned in eternal life
and where folk swim up streams still divided by
railroad tracks
unresolved

once lost now found left
grasping for a Hope who is all
present but unaccounted for in the
interminable slaughter of our
every day

and everybody goes to church as only the
unfaithful would hold a search party just like
no one bothers about those tracks
     because that's just the way things are and not
     everything has a reason no some things are just
     senseless you might even call them stupid like
     when our words aren't more arresting than your
     handcuffs or when the whereabouts of a person's
     humanity remain unknown—

and nobody really preaches about that one story in
the Bible where a sheet falls from the sky filled with
the kinds of creation you never even thought was
food gross reptiles like on those reality tv shows so
peter suddenly wants to fast but here interrupts the voice

of God not because there's a prize to win at the
end but

> because God tells him to get up and kill
> and eat and I don't think God has any problem with
> vegans but the point of the matter is that it is not
> finished;
> see God is still talking and scorns peter for that
> which he despised to make clear that apostle or not
> you have no right to make profane what God has
> called sacred which seems to indicate something
> about where our appetites lie—

and the grammar of incomplete sentences and
incomplete thoughts mean that we incomplete lives
by which incomplete becomes a verb to describe that thing
you do when you cordon off the breath of another human
being before you call your union
representative

> because salvation needs a trigger warning just as
> much as your index finger that maybe it isn't
> really for everyone because some people don't
> deserve to die but maybe do deserve to be shot
> and if death happens to be a consequence of
> their actions then maybe they shouldn't have resisted in
> the first place which would make things so much
> easier for everyone don't you think?—

and it only takes a few stitches to sew sheets into
hoods but it takes four hours to lay one across a
mother's son left to spoil in the street like meat
sacrificed on an altar whose threshold is
melanin's ghost

> because pride cometh before your heartbeat and
> my parking space is more important than your

smile, forgive me it is just human nature the only
continuity of capillaries that matters is mine—

and the blood smeared on doorways won't
stop the blood splattered on sidewalks already
sanctioned in courts as killing fields so they cannot
find a reason to indict and surely have no jurisdiction
to breathe life into bodies not that they would anyway
 because statistics show that if not now then
 eventually when a reason would certainly manifest
 and justify my tracking you down and standing
 my ground against the contents of your character
 which are a disease known for hemorrhaging so
 you have to eat before it eats you
 though of course you already know this
 I saw you flinch when he walked by too—

and there's nothing good about Friday when tears
glue together time that cannot change and will not
wait upon stolen tomorrows
have mercy
 because even if embers of dawn only smolder a
 twilight who leaves bruises in her wake there are
 simply not enough hollow points to stop a
 resistance as fear is illegible to love—

and on days that do not begin with Sun I recall
if I must drown it will not be in a
Lenten sea.

———

## Bread turned to stone: Pietà

LUCI SHAW (naturalized U.S. citizen, contemporary)

Her polished, sculpted arm supports
the marble son, the eyes of Mary
and Jesus both sightless, mouths dumb,
ears sealed to sound, fingers frozen in place.
No hearts under the carved cloth
to pulse and turn again to flesh,
fulfilling Ezekiel. How permanent
is this paralysis? When should we expect
the miracle? How will stone become bread,
become living Word again?

———

## Waiting to Be Filled

EMILY GIBSON (Anglo-American, contemporary)

The call came in the middle of a busy night
as we worked on a floppy baby with high fever,
a croupy toddler whose breathing squeezed and squeaked,
a pale adolescent transfusing due to leukemia bleeding.

It was an anencephalic baby just born, unexpected, unwanted
in a hospital across town, and she needed a place to die.

Our team of three puzzled how to manage a baby without a brain—
simply put her in a room, swaddled, kept warm but alone?
Hydrate her with a dropper of water to moisten her mouth?
Offer her a taste of milk?

She arrived by ambulance, the somber attendants
leaving quickly, unnerved by her mewing cries.

I took the wrapped bundle and peeled away the layers
to find a plump full term baby, her hands gripping, arms waving
once freed;  just another newborn until I pulled off her stocking cap
and looked into an empty crater — only a brainstem lumped at the
    base.

Textbook pictures had not prepared me
for the wholeness, the holiness of this living, breathing child.

Her forehead quit above the eyebrows with the entire skull missing,
tufts of soft brown hair fringed her perfect ears, around the back of
    her neck.
Her eyelids puffy, squinting tight, seemingly too big
above a button nose and rosebud pink lips.

She squirmed under my fingers, her muscles strong, breaths coming
    steady
despite no awareness of light or touch or noise.

Yet she cried in little whimpers, mouth working, seeking,
lips tentatively gripping my fingertip. A bottle warmed,
nipple offered, a tentative suck allowing tiny flow,
then, amazing, a gurgling swallow.

Returning every two hours, more for me than for her, I picked her up
to smell the salty sweet scent of amnion still on her skin as she grew
    dusky.

Her breathing weakened, her muscles loosened, giving up her grip
on a world she would never see or hear or feel to behold
something far more glorious, as I gazed
into her emptiness, waiting to be filled.

———

## *Easter Vigil*
JILL PELÁEZ BAUMGAERTNER (Cuban-American, contemporary)

From the church's side door we follow the candle
held aloft in the uncertain spring evening this dead time
between death and birth, treading the pavement to the opened
narthex door, the procession silent as dusk. Our tapers flare
briefly as they steal flame, then settle into small, steady burns,
each a puncture to the gathered darkness of the sanctuary.

The human story—the rebellions, the redemptions—read
in darkness, the light to some a present shimmer, to most
a dim promise. And you, two brothers, sitting in the deepened
shadows, not quite sure that this hushed service is really
yours, knowing only that your time has almost come.
When the congregation gathers at the font, you stand

shifting your weight, ready now for drowning,
your palms moist. How can this birth be so like death,
you wonder, its public nature almost humiliation?

What happens next is water and movement, then into the fulgent
chancel fragrant with bright narcissus, lily, bread and wine,
the celebration of rising. I recall this now as we awaken
each morning to the stunned wonder of how you could be
one moment and not the next, the child whose forehead once
glistened with sprinkled water, now sunk in the baptism of death.

You know what we do not—the lifting up out of it, the first
gasps of birth, but we linger behind you, words smothered,
motion stopped, lips dry with what we hardly dare believe.

What comes after this vacancy, after the stripped altar
and God's Friday silence? We do not want the cross
the season thrusts upon us. But once again it is our turn.

Our hands cupped, the host pressed into it, the quickening
of the wine, the animating of all from nothing, nuclei, protoplasm—
jellylike, colloidal—the chromosomes, genes, DNA, infused
with movement, tempo, the beating of the heart, the pinking
of the skin, the soft breathing of the sleeper breaking
into wakefulness, eyes opening to effortless light.

———

## Resurrection, imperfect
JOHN DONNE (English, 1572–1631)

Sleep sleep old sun, thou canst not have repassed
As yet, the wound thou took'st on Friday last;
Sleep then, and rest; the world may bear thy stay,
A better sun rose before thee today,
Who, not content to enlighten all that dwell
On the earth's face, as thou, enlightened hell,
And made the dark fires languish in that vale,
As, at thy presence here, our fires grow pale.
Whose body having walked on earth, and now
Hasting to heaven, would, that he might allow
Himself unto all stations, and fill all,
For these three days become a mineral;
He was all gold when he lay down, but rose
All tincture, and doth not alone dispose
Leaden and iron wills to good, but is
Of power to make even sinful flesh like his.
Had one of those, whose credulous piety
Thought, that a soul one might discern and see
Go from a body, at this sepulcher been,
And, issuing from the sheet, this body seen,

He would have justly thought this body a soul,
If not of any man, yet of the whole.
*Desunt cætera.*[24]

———

FROM *Can You See Anything Now*
KATHERINE JAMES (Anglo-American, contemporary)

[Editor's note: In what feels like an effortlessly omniscient voice—as unsentimental yet grace-filled as the gaze of God—James gives us the small New England town of Trinity, where no veneer of wholeness keeps lives together. Instead there is the suicidal painter, Margie, who has been teaching her evangelical neighbor, Etta, how to paint nudes; and Margie's husband, Nick, the town therapist, who suspects his work helps no one; along with their college-aged daughter Noel— whose troubled roommate, Pixie, joined them at home for a winter holiday, only to fall into Trinity's freezing river. That Pixie survived at all is a miracle; months later she is still comatose, attended by her estranged father, Pete, who has become a long-term guest known by the entire town.]

Pete had developed an odd habit, a tick, with his eyes. He would open them as wide as he could in an ocular stretch, and then squeeze them shut. This made him appear at first as though something unexpected had hit his cornea, and then when the process was repeated, two times, three times, he took on that internally crazed appearance that is so indicting of the unstable, like he had a mental itch that he was trying to get at through his eyes. It was hard to say if it was the periodic stretching of his eyes, or his resolute conviction that Pixie would "rise from the dead," that caused the people of Trinity to think he was in need of medication. Nick felt that both were incriminating and that after just a short time talking with Pete, he should refer him to Dr. Lynch as possibly schizophrenic, or at least as having a schizotypal personality disorder, and the doctor could give him a script for Haldol or one of the more recent anti-psychotics.

Nick had finally convinced Pete to come for dinner. Margie remained upstairs with her painting until the last minute, deepening the negative space with an ochre—something that had become difficult to do as the negative space was, it could be argued the more she worked on the painting, actually positive space. The ovens were rounded and thick at the corners. Etta's wipe-out on the other side of the room, with her awkward, slow initial sketches, caught Margie's eye. She looked back at her own painting. There was a softness to the ovens, the rounded corners a nice contrast to the metal-looking ductwork that took right and left turns and angled down from nowhere back into the belly of something like a stove the color of skin. She listened to Nick in the kitchen and glanced out the window from time to time to check for Pete's car.

When she came downstairs Pete was already in the kitchen sitting at a chair pulled away from the table. He held a glass of beer. Nick gave Margie a look.

"Pete," Margie said, "good to see you. I was just finishing up something."

Pete stood up and smiled nervously and then slipped back into his chair.

"We've been talking," Nick said as he dumped a box of fettuccine into boiling water, "about some of the opinions he's getting from Pixie's doctors. . . ."

Margie looked at Pete. "I visited her," she said. "Noel comes home soon and we'll go together. Noel will want to see her."

"Well, that'd be nice. Your friend, Etta, just came to visit. Brought her husband, and some flowers they had. She's been coming all along. Sometimes she prays for Pixie and I appreciate that." Pete widened his eyes and it startled Margie at first. He squeezed them shut. He looked away and then widened them again.

"Religion can really be helpful," Nick said; "Helps you feel grounded. There's a lot to be said for religion. God should be a comfort; God doesn't want to scare you." Nick turned down the burner.

"I light the candles for her."

"He's had different advice from the doctors," Nick said to Margie over his shoulder.

"One of them says let her go," Pete opened his eyes, squeezed them shut. "Go where? That's not up to me, letting her go."

"It's difficult sometimes to think that we might play a role in something this earnest," Nick said.

"Maybe God wants to raise her from the dead."

Nick said, "Well, hmm. . . ."

"What's that to me, if God wants to raise her from the dead?" Pete shrugged and reached for his beer.

"Sometimes we need to take things as they are. . . ."

Pete widened his eyes, squeezed them shut, widened them again.

"Prayer helps us feel in control. . . . It's good for us," Nick said.

"I light the candles. I have a lot of them now. I read a Bible sometimes."

"A great place to start. Try to meditate, center yourself. Do you know what I mean when I say center yourself?"

"I can already feel that. I can feel God and it makes everything back off." Pete finished the last of his beer and set it down hard on the table.

Pete went to Rosedales to make copies. Rosedales was a mailing store where you could register your car or get a notary public or pay a gas bill. There were three parking spaces in front. He had taken a picture of Pixie. He brushed her hair, positioned the camera from above, pressed the button, waited those extra-long seconds for the flash. The camera had cost $39.98 and he had gotten it at Rite Aid. The hard plastic from the packaging fell to the floor next to Pixie's bed. The picture didn't look like her — her face was flat and blank and it looked like her lips were numb and somehow glued together and would need to be peeled apart before she could talk. After taking the picture, Pete had looked at it and been disappointed. He touched her lips and peeled them apart so that her mouth was open. They fell back together. It was her hair. He carefully took the brush and brushed it over her ear and down the side of her face. Static lifted strands into the air when he finished, and he tried to smooth them down again with the palm of his hand. He lifted the camera again, this time keeping it a little to the side. The red dot at his finger lit up, the camera paused, and Pixie's face flashed white with her lips closed and her hair brushed to one side. At Rosedales, a woman helped him make copies of the photograph.

The flyers were everywhere. *See Pixie Rise!* Black and white. The woman had helped Pete print out the words *See Pixie Rise!* with a thick marker, then copy them all off. Fifty. They were stapled to telephone poles and thumb-tacked to bulletin boards in the grocery stores. Taped to benches in the Square. Slid under the wipers of cars.

Spring rain eventually puckered the thin paper, and the images of Pixie took on a new hollowness with the folds. The thick handwritten words moved with the pleating of the paper, fattening and then disappearing, the photograph showing a new twist of the girl's jaw or corrugation of the nose. It was nothing but an image, no more alive than what they were stapled to. Pete went methodically into stores, over to the library, the church, stairwells, bulletin boards, telephone poles and telephone poles, his large hands pressing a staple gun with determined force, as though the pressing itself was an act of love, a way to go backwards.

At the bottom of the flyers it said in small block letters, *July 3, Northeast Rehabilitation Center, 8:00 P.M.*

The white pages lifted at the corners and threatened to become detached. Some did, falling next to curbs, conforming into drains with the rain, clinging to the iron grilles as the paper began its disintegration, softening and then pilling as the pulp began to separate. The hills of Trinity added to the profundity of Pixie's face tacked up on street corners and benches. There was a crying, in a way, the upper streets taking the rain first, sheets of it at times, soaking the papers, pulling at them and then the rivulets of water draining toward Maple. People picked up the soggy papers and sighed, folded them carefully, and threw them away. There was a respect for the flyers, for Pixie's face, that no one would trespass, a reverence for her father, Pete, who continued to post them. Staple gun, large hands, some barely visible beam of hope as he nodded silently to the people he saw on the street.

The paper would dry in its new rain-generated shape, become almost crisp again, and then the rain would come once more, and there the papers would be in the sewer grates, slowly inching their way down the hills. Miriam said, "The whole town is freaking crying."

July 3rd was because it was the day before Independence Day and there would be a natural celebration—a celebration of liberation, the day after Pixie rose from the dead. A parade, fireworks, Pete thought. A day for the wonder of what would happen.

## EASTER SUNDAY

## *Recalled to Life*

OPENING PRAYER

Bearing our curse, becoming sin,
You loose us from both the burden
of the law and from our lawlessness.
You bruise the serpent's head,
and snatch us from its grip. You open
the way to resurrection, shattering
the gates of hell. You slay the one
who held death's power, give comfort
to those who honor You. You give the holy cross
by which our enemy is slain, by which
our life returns to us abundantly.
—MACRINA THE YOUNGER (Turkish, ca. 327–379)
adapted by Scott Cairns

SCRIPTURES

PSALM 116 | AMOS 9:11–15 | ROMANS 6:1–11 | JOHN 20:1–18

READINGS

"Rosing from the Dead" by PAUL J. WILLIS
"After the Funeral They Bring Food" by JEANNE MURRAY WALKER
"Sunday" by HANNAH FAITH NOTESS
"Easter" by GEORGE HERBERT
"Easter" by BENJAMÍN ALIRE SÁENZ
From *Can You See Anything Now* by KATHERINE JAMES

PERSONAL PRAYER AND REFLECTION

CLOSING PRAYER

Thou'rt born, and, lo, bright King, thy world is born,
Is born with thee from virgin tomb this morn.
Hastes Nature to its second day of birth,
And a new life in thee crowns a new earth.
Dear Sun, from thy life all things draw life's breath;
Nought thence is forced to die, save only Death.
Nor is Death forced—since in thy grave to lie,
Death will itself, O Christ, be glad to die.
—RICHARD CRASHAW (English, 1612–1649)

# READINGS

## Rosing from the Dead
PAUL J. WILLIS (Anglo-American, contemporary)

We are on our way home
from Good Friday service.
It is dark. It is silent.
"Sunday," says Hanna,
"Jesus will be rosing
from the dead."

It must have been like that.
A white blossom, or maybe
a red one, pulsing
from the floor of the tomb, reaching
round the Easter stone
and levering it aside
with pliant thorns.

The soldiers overcome
with the fragrance,
and Mary at sunrise
mistakening the dawn-dewed
Rose of Sharon
for the untameable Gardener.

———

## After the Funeral They Bring Food
JEANNE MURRAY WALKER (Anglo-American, contemporary)

His friend Martha's making soup, because you still
have to eat. Meanwhile, back in the Garden

cave, the same Garden where he prayed to let
this cup pass from him, He comes to Himself a weight

on a stone shelf in the cool dark, all 200 pounds
of Him, only changed. Minus mass, maybe,

or impervious to gravity. He doesn't understand this
as a physics problem. He lifts his hand and stares

at it. In town Martha's lightheaded, and trying to keep
her tears out of the soup. The cabbage offers her

its tough pale green handles to hold onto. She strips
its layers down to the heart, while Jesus—his face

astonished—chisel it in marble!—lasers through
the swaddling grave clothes. Heaven's volatile physics

draws him up. In the deepest dark of winter
when I hold a cabbage, peel off its outer leaves,

before I plunge the knife in, I think, when I take
the final journey, I'll have this green moon to light the way.

## Sunday

HANNAH FAITH NOTESS (Anglo-American, contemporary)

In the garden, a girl waits
for what she has seen to make sense.
It was too early, hardly light.
The clouds had not parted, no sun
lit the water-beaded spiderwebs
to weave them into a glittering shawl.

In the garden, the girl remembers
the room felt as though someone
had just walked out, and it smelled
not of incense, but of earth,
not of balm or spices, but the rust
in the clay that tastes of blood.

In the garden, she listens
to the steady drop of rain on leaf.
And as the wind unfurls the sweet
breath of stem and petal,
the garden begins to smell
like the kingdom of heaven.

In the garden, no one will ask her
to give up grief altogether,
not yet. But a man will say
her name, as though her name
could answer any question,

and she will say nothing to anyone
because what she has seen
is cold and clear as water
running over the hands of a blind girl
before she was made to see.

## *Easter*

GEORGE HERBERT (English, 1593–1633)

### I.

Rise heart; thy Lord is risen. Sing his praise
                    Without delays,
Who takes thee by the hand, that thou likewise
                    With him mayst rise:
That, as his death calcined thee to dust,
His life may make thee gold, and much more just.

Awake, my lute, and struggle for thy part
                    With all thy art.
The cross taught all wood to resound his name,
                    Who bore the same.
His stretched sinews taught all strings, what key
Is best to celebrate this most high day.

Consort both heart and lute, and twist a song
                    Pleasant and long:
Or since all music is but three parts vied
                    And multiplied;
O let thy blessed Spirit bear a part,
And make up our defects with his sweet art.

### II.

I got me flowers to straw thy way;
I got me boughs off many a tree:
But thou wast up by break of day,
And brought'st thy sweets along with thee.

The Sun arising in the East,
Though he give light, and th' East perfume;
If they should offer to contest
With thy arising, they presume.

Can there be any day but this,
Though many suns to shine endeavor?
We count three hundred, but we miss:
There is but one, and that one ever.

———

## *Easter*

BENJAMÍN ALIRE SÁENZ (Mexican-American, contemporary)

> *Mesilla, New Mexico*
> *Spring, 1962*

My mother woke us that Sunday—her voice
a bell proclaiming spring. We rose
diving into our clothes, newly bought.
We took turns standing before mirrors,
combing, staring at our new selves.
Sinless from forty days of desert,
sinless from good confessions, we
drove to church in a red pickup, bright
and red and waxed for the special
occasion. Clean, polished as apples,
the yellow-dressed girls in front
with Mom and Dad; the boys in back,
our hair blowing free in the warming
wind. Winter gone away. At Mass,
the choir singing loud: ragged
notes from ragged angels' voices;
ancient hymns sung in crooked Latin.
The priest, white-robed, raised his palms
toward God, opened his mouth in awe:
"Alleluia!" The unspoken word of Lent

let loose in flight. Alleluia and incense
rising, my mother wiping her tears
from words she'd heard; my brother and I
whispering names of statues lining
the walls of the church. Bells ringing,
Mass ending, we running to the truck,
shiny as shoes going dancing. Dad
driving us to see my grandmother. There,
at her house, I asked about the new word
I'd heard: *resurrection.* "Death,
death," she said, her hands moving downward,
"the cross—*that* is death." And then she
laughed: "The dead will rise." Her upturned
palms moved skyward as she spoke. "The dead
will rise." She moved her hands toward me,
wrapped my face with touches, and
laughed again. *The dead will rise.*

———

FROM *Can You See Anything Now*
KATHERINE JAMES (Anglo-American, contemporary)

[Editor's note: July 3rd has come and gone in the New England town
of Trinity, and comatose Pixie did not "rise from the dead," as her
father, Pete, had hoped. But James' epilogue changes everything.]

To wake up meant that Pixie would have to push something up
to the surface and be able to focus on it. It required a physical
cognition that she hadn't used for some time, and so when it was too
late to back out, she got up the nerve and let go of what had been
so lovingly pulling at her soul and concentrated on her father in the
chair with his head bowed wanting to change something but unable
to. This helped.

She lifted two fingers. That's all, just the fingers. Nothing. It was all in the eyes though, she discovered, as she was able to open them for a second or two. Big bang for the buck: Pete looked at her, caught his breath, stood up, leaned over the bed and pushed something. Ah, now we have contact. She opened them once more, caught his eyes, and closed them.

What a glorious bustle of life, the little room with the metal bed and synthetic hospital equipment. Nurses don't wear white anymore, they opt for patterns suited, it seemed to Pixie, for their personalities. Mickey and Minnie. Balloons. Was she in a pediatric ward? Pete put his large warm hand to her cheek and her eyes welled up even though she didn't feel sad or happy, and tears ran down the side of her face and into her ears. The feeling was like zippers opening. She could breathe. She was taped together in various places, needles stuck into her with tubes and juice and lines leading to things. A thin tube ran over one of her thighs and out from under the sheet. The tube grew warm and then cool again. Her mouth, oh, her mouth and her throat, she hadn't thought about her mouth. She was in, she was out, she drifted back to sleep.

There was a line from a song by Devendra Banhart that kept repeating in Pixie's mind when she awoke again to her father sitting next to her and someone sponging her forehead. *We see things like this*, someone said at least three times, as though it was such an honor and somehow worth bragging about. The song was about something she couldn't quite remember, except one line, *And let regret end at the start of the day.* The first intentional thought Pixie had was to figure out the song, there was more to it, but all she had was that one line. She needed to get right on that, but with all of the activity and then the two doctors—or the one doctor with the student, it was hard to tell— she barely had time to take her first official breath of mortal air. Pete had lost weight. He looked starved, like he'd been eating applesauce for months. The front of his shirt had a stain and it reminded Pixie of a commercial that has a woman with a bottle of laundry detergent… there's some sort of white room and children playing. People detached various things from her body. Somebody, the student intern or the doctor's sidekick, pulled a lamp on a long metal arm out from the wall. Her father looked at her like he was holding his breath. He bent over and kissed her on the forehead. What was that? There was so much she did not understand, but in a way it didn't matter. She slowly raised one of her knees and then lowered it. Oh, the control, the outrageous control. And now the biggest thing, to speak, but she would wait: this, she knew, would take time. It was the consonants she worried about, they would be difficult. Someone ran water into a sink. There was a shadow of people gathered outside the door in the hallway but they didn't talk. One of them came in the room and Pete turned to look. He got up and hugged the shadow and the shadow came to the foot of the bed and then she was very light, it turned out, her hair was bright and curled under, and there was a necklace hanging from her neck and it was almost as though she knew Pixie, the way she stood there and smiled, but it wasn't a smirky smile, it was a real smile and Pixie would make a note of this, that the woman with the nice, bright hair and the necklace could be trusted. Then she remembered the song: *And let regret end at the start of the day / …don't take no secrets back to your grave / let everyone know, let everyone know.* She slowly folded her arms under the sheet and ran her hands along her upper arms because this is something she used to do, and there they still were, all the scars lined up like words. She felt the soft ridges and played them with her fingers, but even though they were still there it was like feeling light because that was another world and another life. She remembered the name of the song, *Angelika,* it was called. She was pretty sure of this.

# EASTERTIDE WEEK 1

## The Place of Consolation

OPENING PRAYER
Eternal One, Almighty Trine![25]
(Since thou art ours, and we are thine,)
By all thy love did once resign,

By all the grace thy heavens still hide,
We pray thee, keep us at thy side,
Creator, Savior, strengthening Guide!
—JOHN KEBLE (English, 1792–1866)

SCRIPTURES
PSALM 23 | MICAH 7:4–20 | ROMANS 6:12–23 | JOHN 21:9–19

READINGS
"Easter Monday" by CHRISTINA ROSSETTI
"We Take the Sky" by SUSANNA CHILDRESS
"Vespers" by DERRICK AUSTIN
"John 21" by KATHERINE JAMES
"…for they shall see God" by LUCI SHAW
"As If There Were Only One" by MARTHA SERPAS
From *The Light Princess* by GEORGE MACDONALD

PERSONAL PRAYER AND REFLECTION

CLOSING PRAYER
O let me, when thy roof my soul hath hid,
O let me roost and nestle there:

Then of a sinner thou art rid,
And I of hope and fear.
—GEORGE HERBERT (English, 1593–1633)

## READINGS

## Easter Monday
CHRISTINA ROSSETTI (English, 1830–1894)

Out in the rain a world is growing green,
  On half the trees quick buds are seen
    Where glued-up buds have been.
Out in the rain God's Acre stretches green,
  Its harvest quick tho' still unseen:
    For there the Life hath been.

If Christ hath died His brethren well may die,
  Sing in the gate of death, lay by
    This life without a sigh:
For Christ hath died and good it is to die;
  To sleep whenso He lays us by,
    Then wake without a sigh.

Yea, Christ hath died, yea, Christ is risen again:
  Wherefore both life and death grow plain
    To us who wax and wane;
For Christ Who rose shall die no more again:
  Amen: till He makes all things plain
    Let us wax on and wane.

## We Take the Sky

SUSANNA CHILDRESS (Anglo-American, contemporary)

We take the sky, as if red is something we could own,
something we might find in the stillest moments,
as if the earth is humane and wouldn't break
our bones. (None of His were broken. Not one.)

Red is in the land too, is in the way we look at each other, the hardness
of our sleep, the need to fall down, to tell of the pox that swept Aunt
  Jess,
the drink that ushers Father, the path that never leads to wealth or rest
or health—but the one we always take. *Shalom*, we say. *Buena suerte.*[26]

We always take the sky, fold it over ourselves,
the soil, run it across our skin and cling to it,
savoring the tart of a lemon, palming a bar of soap
even when our hands are clean, naming the insects

that fly across the white bulb of moon late at night,
rakishly loving the one who knows our smell,
saying (as if they are not questions), *Isn't this how
we stay alive* and *Why shouldn't I burrow here.*

This is how we drum on, cold and ungrowing—
what more to be than alive? It all hums: so we die in small bits,
so the egg-shaped hollow that sits behind our stomachs,
so He died and rose again on the third day, so (what).

We take the sky, we scatter on the land. We fall down,
grab the everythings, the tiniest cures, fall down again,
wash ourselves in red and know, unwittingly, it is not enough.
More certain than anything: it will never be,

and then here, in the stillest moments, the story rushes again
(veil splitting, stone rolling, Mary, Peter, John, running,

linen and spices like a limp cocoon, the blur of angels, the one red
splash of a second—like a rose breaking open—when we know),

and somewhere inside us a small green seed pricks the dirt,
coiling for air. He soothes and stirs, fingertip-sized holes in His
hands, roaming the soil and the sky for our broken bones.
And the shaking on earth is our brand new lives:

*Alleluia*, we say, feeling even the empty oval of our stomachs rise.

———

## Vespers
DERRICK AUSTIN (African-American, contemporary)

Lord in the pigment, the crushed, colored stones.
Lord in the carved marble chest. I turn away
from art. You are between my eye and what I see.
Forgive my errant gaze. Tonight, I can't sleep
and won't frighten the deer in my peonies.
Like children who rub their grimy hands over everything,
they only want to touch and be touched by grass.
They've never known violence, cars howling out of darkness.
Lord in the camellia, drifting in and out of sight,
like those blushing, perfumed heads will you welcome me?
I, too, am little more than a stranger in your garden.
Stroke my velvety antlers. Open your palms.

———

## John 21
KATHERINE JAMES (Anglo-American, contemporary)

Poignant musht[27]
in a balm of fishy-charcoal,

sand still cold
from the night.

The charred wood
could write volumes on the hearts
of 12, no, 11 men in tunics,
veins busting from skin salty
with ocean and sweat.

The loved one cannot write
the words, though
try as he does. It's the smell
of morning and the peopled
wooden boat that prevent him;
anything white becomes
radiant in early dawn.

He hangs back
and listens to words
exchanged that will travel
centuries, and even then settle uneven
in the hearts of men.

It's all too wonderful
to expect such things,
but he must,
so he chooses the
third person

as though he were someone else.

———

## "...for they shall see God"

LUCI SHAW (naturalized U.S. citizen, contemporary)

*Matthew 5:8*

Christ risen was rarely
recognized by sight.
They had to get beyond the way he looked.
Evidence stronger than
his voice and face and footstep
waited to grow in them, to guide
their groping from despair,
their stretching toward belief.

We are as blind as they
until the opening of our deeper eyes
shows us the hands that bless
and break our bread,
until we finger
wounds that tell our healing,
or witness a miracle of fish
dawn-caught after our long night
of empty nets. Handling
his Word, we feel his flesh,
his bones, and hear his voice
calling our early-morning name.

———

## As If There Were Only One

MARTHA SERPAS (Anglo-American, contemporary)

In the morning God pulled me onto the porch,
a rain-washed gray and brilliant shore.

I sat in my orange pajamas and waited.
God said, "Look at that tree." And I did.

Its leaves were newly yellow and green,
slick and bright, and so alive it hurt

to take the colors in. My pupils grew
hungry and wide against my will.

God said, "Listen to the tree."
And I did. It said, "Live!"

And it opened itself wider, not with desire,
but the way I imagine a surgeon spreads

the ribs of a patient in distress and rubs
her paralyzed heart, only this tree parted

its own limbs toward the sky—I was the light in that sky.
I reached in to the thick, sweet core

and I lifted it to my mouth and held it there
for a long time until I tasted the word

*tree* (because I had forgotten its name).
Then I said my own name twice softly.

Augustine said, *God loves each of us as if
there were only one of us,* but I hadn't believed him.

And God put me down on the steps with my coffee
and my cigarettes. And, although I still

could not eat nor sleep, that evening
and that morning were my first day back.

———

FROM *The Light Princess*
GEORGE MACDONALD (Scottish, 1824–1905)

[Editor's note: We pick up MacDonald's fairytale where we left off, bearing witness to the princess's transformation.]

. . . The princess gave a shriek, and sprang into the lake.

She laid hold first of one leg, and then of the other, and pulled and tugged, but she could not move either. She stopped to take breath, and that made her think that *he* could not get any breath. She was frantic. She got hold of him, and held his head above the water, which was possible now his hands were no longer on the hole. But it was of no use, for he was past breathing.

Love and water brought back all her strength. She got under the water, and pulled and pulled with her whole might, till at last she got one leg out. The other easily followed. How she got him into the boat she never could tell; but when she did, she fainted away. Coming to herself, she seized the oars, kept herself steady as best she could, and rowed and rowed, though she had never rowed before. Round rocks, and over shallows, and through mud she rowed, till she got to the landing-stairs of the palace. By this time her people were on the shore, for they had heard her shriek. She made them carry the prince to her own room, and lay him in her bed, and light a fire, and send for the doctors.

"But the lake, your Highness!" said the chamberlain, who, roused by the noise, came in, in his nightcap.

"Go and drown yourself in it!" she said.

This was the last rudeness of which the princess was ever guilty; and one must allow that she had good cause to feel provoked with the lord chamberlain.

Had it been the king himself, he would have fared no better. But both he and the queen were fast asleep. And the chamberlain went back to his bed. Somehow, the doctors never came. So the princess and her old nurse were left with the prince. But the old nurse was a wise woman, and knew what to do.

They tried everything for a long time without success. The princess was nearly distracted between hope and fear, but she tried on and on, one thing after another, and everything over and over again.

At last, when they had all but given it up, just as the sun rose, the prince opened his eyes. . . .

. . . The princess burst into a passion of tears, and fell on the floor. There she lay for an hour, and her tears never ceased. All the pent-up crying of her life was spent now. And a rain came on, such as had never been seen in that country. The sun shone all the time, and the great drops, which fell straight to the earth, shone likewise. The palace was in the heart of a rainbow. It was a rain of rubies, and sapphires, and emeralds, and topazes. The torrents poured from the mountains like molten gold; and if it had not been for its subterraneous outlet, the lake would have overflowed and inundated the country. It was full from shore to shore.

But the princess did not heed the lake. She lay on the floor and wept, and this rain within doors was far more wonderful than the rain out of doors.

For when it abated a little, and she proceeded to rise, she found, to her astonishment, that she could not. At length, after many efforts, she succeeded in getting upon her feet. But she tumbled down again directly. Hearing her fall, her old nurse uttered a yell of delight, and ran to her, screaming,—

"My darling child! She's found her gravity!"

"Oh, that's it! is it?" said the princess, rubbing her shoulder and her knee alternately. "I consider it very unpleasant. I feel as if I should be crushed to pieces."

"Hurrah!" cried the prince from the bed. "If you've come round, princess, so have I. How's the lake?"

"Brimful," answered the nurse.

"Then we're all happy."

"That we are indeed!" answered the princess, sobbing.

And there was rejoicing all over the country that rainy day. Even the babies forgot their past troubles, and danced and crowed amazingly. And the king told stories, and the queen listened to them. And he divided the money in his box, and she the honey in her pot, among all the children. And there was such jubilation as was never heard of before.

Of course the prince and princess were betrothed at once. But the princess had to learn to walk, before they could be married with any propriety. And this was not so easy at her time of life, for she could walk no more than a baby. She was always falling down and hurting herself.

"Is this the gravity you used to make so much of?" said she one day to the prince, as he raised her from the floor. "For my part, I was a great deal more comfortable without it."

"No, no, that's not it. This is it," replied the prince, as he took her up, and carried her about like a baby, kissing her all the time. "This is gravity."

"That's better," said she. "I don't mind that so much."

And she smiled the sweetest, loveliest smile in the prince's face. And she gave him one little kiss in return for all his; and he thought them overpaid, for he was beside himself with delight. I fear she complained of her gravity more than once after this, notwithstanding.

It was a long time before she got reconciled to walking. But the pain of learning it was quite counterbalanced by two things, either of which would have been sufficient consolation. The first was, that the prince himself was her teacher; and the second, that she could tumble into the lake as often as she pleased. Still, she preferred to have the prince jump in with her; and the splash they made before was nothing to the splash they made now.

# EASTERTIDE WEEK 2

## *Undeserved Deliverance*

### OPENING PRAYER

lord
do you want to remain the eternally unavailable one?
or do you grow with my prayer?
then reveal yourself also to the beggar
beneath the undivided heavens
and to the stray mare under the shelter
be path be night
until walking in the light i fall into the snare
—SAID (Iranian, contemporary)

### SCRIPTURES
PSALM 18 | ISAIAH 12 | ROMANS 8:1–11 | JOHN 20:19–29

### READINGS
"Bloodline" by LUCI SHAW
"Starting Over" by MARY F. C. PRATT
"Let me be to Thee" by GERARD MANLEY HOPKINS
"Banding" by SUZANNE UNDERWOOD RHODES
From *Robinson Crusoe* by DANIEL DEFOE

### PERSONAL PRAYER AND REFLECTION

### CLOSING PRAYER
O Holy Ghost, whose temple I
Am, but of mud walls, and condensed dust,
    And being sacrilegiously
Half wasted with youth's fires, of pride and lust,
    Must with new storms be weatherbeat;

Double in my heart thy flame,
Which let devout sad tears intend; and let
(Though this glass lanthorn,[28] flesh, do suffer maim)
Fire, sacrifice, priest, altar be the same.
—JOHN DONNE (English, 1572–1631)

READINGS

## Bloodline

LUCI SHAW (naturalized U.S. Citizen, contemporary)

All it takes is a simple incursion, some sharp sever.
A jag. An abrupt disclosure—the secret fluid
spills against its will! Whether a startle or slow
seepage, a prompt to own our vulnerability.

But the extravagant fertility of blood! How
dependably it pumps, breeding itself in the marrow
to re-fill what drains away, the rivers of bright
platelets singing in their arterial dark.

When an old splash above a door in Egypt became
a shield, a lifeguard against the death angel, it was only
a lamb; *we* didn't have to die. A quick throat cut
flooded us with a forgiveness that freed us to escape.

"His blood be upon us" echoes in that old yell of
enraged rejection. Now, as we yield ourselves to be
washed in grace's laundry, the scandal of undeserved
mercy acts on us as God's unlikely bleach.

Today the cup calls us to the rail, speaks
in the same lambent, exculpatory voice, transfuses us

through its deep drinking, a stain that
blots old grimes and dyes us with itself.

———

## Starting Over
MARY F. C. PRATT (Anglo-American, contemporary)

—and do you remember the night the long rain stopped?
We woke to silence, and moonlight through the high window.
No sound but the animals breathing in their sleep—
—and the owls—

It was so hard to wait
but when the dove did not return
you worked open the swollen latch
and we pushed the ladder out.
I shooed away the chickens—
all those chickens underfoot.

You insisted on going first
even though your rheumatism was bad—
and I came down right behind you
with my knees not so much better.
Soft wet dirt, all the swamp stink,
but not a cloud in sight.

On top of the hill, that one tree
—Olive—with little leaves unfolding,
beginnings of buds where new olives would be—

The children crowded down behind.
Everything that could fly flew;
and the mice and monkeys, squirrels, possums,
horses, camels, cats and dogs.

Stones everywhere, like bones;
and bones, so many bones.

I scattered the seeds I'd saved on the slick and blackened ground.
You made a pile of stones, went back in and fetched a lamb, a calf.
The sun warmed my face—
We brought fire from the little lamp
while the bow shimmered there, hanging there—

Somehow the freedom of it—
so strange even now remembering it, believing it—
knowing that we are the ones—
the making and mending, the losing, yielding,
how it all comes out—

So soon the olives bloomed, blossoms fell,
little seeds grew up to grain.
We made wine from the grapes;
apples ripened red, so sweet,
on every clean-picked twig the nub of next year's fruit;
in each white heart one strange and impeccable star.

———

## 'Let me be to Thee'
GERARD MANLEY HOPKINS (English, 1844–1889)

Let me be to Thee as the circling bird,
Or bat with tender and air-crisping wings
That shapes in half-light his departing rings,
From both of whom a changeless note is heard.
I have found my music in a common word,
Trying each pleasurable throat that sings
And every praiséd sequence of sweet strings,
And know infallibly which I preferred.

The authentic cadence was discovered late
Which ends those only strains that I approve,
And other science all gone out of date
And minor sweetness scarce made mention of:
I have found the dominant of my range and state—
Love, O my God, to call Thee Love and Love.

———

## Banding
SUZANNE UNDERWOOD RHODES (Anglo-American, contemporary)

The nets of God hang in every wild place
to catch the unwary migrant, one with the skull
another to fall from the sky on the ten-thousandth mile,

but when he holds one of those small, terrified
bodies like a jewel between his thumb and forefinger
and unfans the wing to measure it, secretly admiring
the bars he conceived to catch his own hungry eye,
and the little claw foot he rings with a coded band
that numbers the feathers and weds him forever
to the pulse in his palm that recalls his own heaving heart
the day he flew into a net and hung there thirsting
in the woods where only a wasp moved, flicking cobalt wings,

when he lets go, when he flings what he has marked
into emptiness, he follows the speck with his eye
to South America and farther, to white, unmapped fields
known intimately in the mind of those who fly.

———

From *Robinson Crusoe*
DANIEL DEFOE (English, 1660–1731)

[Editor's note: Pick the most rebellious, wandering soul you know—
prideful, selfish, risk-seeking, risk-taking, deliberately errant—and
that's Robinson Crusoe, Defoe's invented adventurer. More than half
of the tale follows Crusoe's first-person account of his seafaring es-
capades, skirmishes, and narrow escapes; but then eventually he is
stranded on a deserted island, and that's when things, as they say, get
real. After many long months, Crusoe becomes violently ill, facing his
own mortality, and finally awakens to his true spiritual condition. We
pick up his journal there.]

I had no more sense of God or His judgments—much less of the
present affliction of my circumstances being from His hand—
than if I had been in the most prosperous condition of life. But now,
when I began to be sick, and a leisurely view of the miseries of death
came to place itself before me; when my spirits began to sink under
the burden of a strong distemper, and nature was exhausted with
the violence of the fever; conscience, that had slept so long, began to
awake, and I began to reproach myself with my past life, in which I
had so evidently, by uncommon wickedness, provoked the justice of
God to lay me under uncommon strokes, and to deal with me in so
vindictive a manner. These reflections oppressed me for the second
or third day of my distemper; and in the violence, as well of the
fever as of the dreadful reproaches of my conscience, extorted some
words from me like praying to God, though I cannot say they were
either a prayer attended with desires or with hopes: it was rather the
voice of mere fright and distress. My thoughts were confused, the
convictions great upon my mind, and the horror of dying in such
a miserable condition raised vapors into my head with the mere
apprehensions; and in these hurries of my soul I knew not what my
tongue might express. But it was rather exclamation, such as, "Lord,
what a miserable creature am I! If I should be sick, I shall certainly

die for want of help; and what will become of me!" Then the tears burst out of my eyes, and I could say no more for a good while. In this interval the good advice of my father came to my mind, and presently his prediction, which I mentioned at the beginning of this story—viz., that if I did take this foolish step, God would not bless me, and I would have leisure hereafter to reflect upon having neglected his counsel when there might be none to assist in my recovery. "Now," said I, aloud, "my dear father's words are come to pass; God's justice has overtaken me, and I have none to help or hear me. I rejected the voice of Providence, which had mercifully put me in a posture or station of life wherein I might have been happy and easy; but I would neither see it myself nor learn to know the blessing of it from my parents. I left them to mourn over my folly, and now I am left to mourn under the consequences of it. I abused their help and assistance, who would have lifted me in the world, and would have made everything easy to me; and now I have difficulties to struggle with, too great for even nature itself to support, and no assistance, no help, no comfort, no advice." Then I cried out, "Lord, be my help, for I am in great distress." This was the first prayer, if I may call it so, that I had made for many years...

...In the interval of this operation I took up the Bible and began to read; but my head was too much disturbed with the tobacco to bear reading, at least at that time; only, having opened the book casually, the first words that occurred to me were these, "Call on Me in the day of trouble, and I will deliver thee, and thou shalt glorify Me." These words were very apt to my case, and made some impression upon my thoughts at the time of reading them, though not so much as they did afterwards; for, as for being *delivered*, the word had no sound, as I may say, to me; the thing was so remote, so impossible in my apprehension of things, that I began to say, as the children of Israel did when they were promised flesh to eat, "Can God spread a table in the wilderness?" so I began to say, "Can God Himself deliver me from this place?" And as it was not for many years that any hopes appeared, this prevailed very often upon my thoughts; but, however, the words made a great impression upon me, and I mused upon them very often. It grew now late, and the tobacco had, as I said, dozed my head so much that I inclined to sleep; so I left my lamp burning in the cave, lest I should want anything in the night, and went to bed. But before I lay down, I did what I never had done in all my life—I kneeled down, and prayed to God to fulfill the promise to me, that if I called upon Him in the day of trouble, He would deliver me. . . .

. . . *July 3.*—. . . I did not recover my full strength for some weeks after. While I was thus gathering strength, my thoughts ran exceedingly upon this Scripture, "I will deliver thee"; and the impossibility of my deliverance lay much upon my mind, in bar of my ever expecting it; but as I was discouraging myself with such thoughts, it occurred to my mind that I pored so much upon my deliverance from the main affliction, that I disregarded the deliverance I had received, and I was as it were made to ask myself such questions as these—viz., Have I not been delivered, and wonderfully too, from sickness—from the most distressed condition that could be, and that was so frightful to me? And what notice had I taken of it? Had I done my part? God had delivered me, but I had not glorified Him—that is to say, I had not owned and been thankful for that as a deliverance; and how could I expect greater deliverance? This touched my heart very much; and immediately I knelt down and gave God thanks aloud for my recovery from my sickness.

*July* 4.—In the morning I took the Bible; and beginning at the New Testament, I began seriously to read it, and imposed upon myself to read a while every morning and every night; not tying myself to the number of chapters, but long as my thoughts should engage me. It was not long after I set seriously to this work till I found my heart more deeply and sincerely affected with the wickedness of my past life. The impression of my dream revived; and the words, "All these things have not brought thee to repentance," ran seriously through my thoughts. I was earnestly begging of God to give me repentance, when it happened providentially, the very day, that, reading the Scripture, I came to these words: "He is exalted a Prince and a Savior, to give repentance and to give remission." I threw down the book; and with my heart as well as my hands lifted up to heaven, in a kind of ecstasy of joy, I cried out aloud, "Jesus, thou son of David! Jesus, thou exalted Prince and Savior! give me repentance!" This was the first time I could say, in the true sense of the words, that I prayed in all my life; for now I prayed with a sense of my condition, and a true Scripture view of hope, founded on the encouragement of the Word of God; and from this time, I may say, I began to hope that God would hear me.

Now I began to construe the words mentioned above, "Call on Me, and I will deliver thee," in a different sense from what I had ever done before; for then I had no notion of anything being called *deliverance*, but my being delivered from the captivity I was in; for though I was indeed at large in the place, yet the island was certainly a prison to me, and that in the worse sense in the world. But now I learned to take it in another sense: now I looked back upon my past life with such horror, and my sins appeared so dreadful, that my soul sought nothing of God but deliverance from the load of guilt that bore down all my comfort. As for my solitary life, it was nothing. I did not so much as pray to be delivered from it or think of it; it was all of no consideration in comparison to this. And I add this part here, to hint to whoever shall read it, that whenever they come to a true sense of things, they will find deliverance from sin a much greater blessing than deliverance from affliction.

## EASTERTIDE WEEK 3

---

# *The Way of Affirmation*

OPENING PRAYER

Let us rejoice, O my Beloved!
Let us go forth to see ourselves in Your beauty,
To the mountain and the hill,
Where the pure water flows:
Let us enter into the heart of the thicket.
—JOHN OF THE CROSS (Spanish, 1542–1591)

SCRIPTURES

PSALM 16 | ISAIAH 58:6–12 | ROMANS 8:12–17 | LUKE 24:13–35 |

READINGS

"The Good Portion" by PAUL J. WILLIS
"The Windhover" by GERARD MANLEY HOPKINS
"Spring Beholding" by MARY F. C. PRATT
"Creed" by ABIGAIL CARROLL
"Past and Future" by ELIZABETH BARRETT BROWNING
From *Middlemarch* by GEORGE ELIOT (A.K.A., MARY ANNE EVANS)

PERSONAL PRAYER AND REFLECTION

CLOSING PRAYER

Gloriously wasteful, O my Lord, art thou!
Sunset faints after sunset into the night,
Splendorously dying from thy window sill—
For ever. Sad our poverty doth bow
Before the riches of thy making might:

Sweep from thy space thy systems at thy will—
In thee the sun sets every sunset still.
— GEORGE MACDONALD (Scottish, 1824–1905)

## READINGS

### *The Good Portion*
PAUL J. WILLIS (Anglo-American, contemporary)

> *Mary has chosen the good portion, which shall not be
> taken away from her.* Luke 10:42

Is it waking to this calm morning
after a night of dry winds?

Is it scrambled eggs, the ones with cheese,
or the hot glaze of a cinnamon roll?

Is it the way you laugh over breakfast,
that generous gift, your laughter?

Is it rinsing the plates and pans in the sink?
Or leaving them in a cockeyed stack,

these things of use, these things of beauty
that will not be taken away?

———

## The Windhover
GERARD MANLEY HOPKINS (English, 1844–1889)

> To Christ our Lord

I caught this morning morning's minion, king-
    dom of daylight's dauphin, dapple-dawn-drawn Falcon, in his
      riding
Of the rolling level underneath him steady air, and striding
High there, how he rung upon the rein of a wimpling wing
In his ecstasy! then off, off forth on swing,
    As a skate's heel sweeps smooth on a bow-bend: the hurl and
      gliding
Rebuffed the big wind. My heart in hiding
Stirred for a bird, —the achieve of, the mastery of the thing!

Brute beauty and valor and act, oh, air, pride, plume, here
    Buckle! AND the fire that breaks from thee then, a billion
Times told lovelier, more dangerous, O my chevalier!

    No wonder of it: sheer plod makes plough down sillion
Shine, and blue-bleak embers, ah my dear,
    Fall, gall themselves, and gash gold-vermilion.

————

## Spring Beholding
MARY F. C. PRATT (Anglo-American, contemporary)

> *The fullness of joy is to behold God in everything.*
> —Julian of Norwich

Otter washing her paws
in the cold pond water.

Bluebird, robin, forgotten
songs come home.

Vulture and hawk
soaring the slope.

Three thin deer,
feet splayed in dry grass.

Squirrels. Rabbits.
Stones.

Snowmelt, icy
from the hills.

Logging truck grunting
far down the road,

its work, its purpose,
its heavy load.

————

## Creed

ABIGAIL CARROLL (Anglo-American, contemporary)

I believe in the life of the word,
the diplomacy of food. I believe in salt-thick
ancient seas and the absoluteness of blue.
A poem is an ark, a suitcase in which to pack
the universe—I believe in the universality
of art, of human thirst

for a place. I believe in Adam's work
of naming breath and weather—all manner
of wind and stillness, humidity
and heat. I believe in the audacity
of light, the patience of cedars,
the innocence of weeds. I believe

in apologies, soliloquies, speaking
in tongues; the underwater
operas of whales, the secret
prayer rituals of bees. As for miracles—
the perfection of cells, the integrity
of wings—I believe. Bones

know the dust from which they come;
all music spins through space on just
a breath. I believe in that grand economy
of love that counts the tiny death
of every fern and white-tailed fox.
I believe in the healing ministry

of phlox, the holy brokenness of saints,
the fortuity of faults—of making
and then redeeming mistakes. Who dares
brush off the auguries of a storm, disdain
the lilting eulogies of the moon? To dance
is nothing less than an act of faith

in what the prophets sang. I believe
in the genius of children and the goodness
of sleep, the eternal impulse to create. For love
of God and the human race, I believe
in the elegance of insects, the imminence
of winter, the free enterprise of grace.

———

## Past and Future

ELIZABETH BARRETT BROWNING (English, 1806–1861)

My future will not copy fair my past
On any leaf but Heaven's. Be fully done

Supernal Will! I would not fain be one
Who, satisfying thirst and breaking fast,
Upon the fulness of the heart at last
Says no grace after meat. My wine has run
Indeed out of my cup, and there is none
To gather up the bread of my repast
Scattered and trampled; yet I find some good
In earth's green herbs, and streams that bubble up
Clear from the darkling ground,—content until
I sit with angels before better food:—
Dear Christ! when thy new vintage fills my cup,
This hand shall shake no more, nor that wine spill.

———

## From *Middlemarch*

GEORGE ELIOT (a.k.a., Mary Anne Evans, English, 1819–1880)

[Editor's note: Much to the surprise of her family and friends, the earnest, pious, good-hearted Dorothea Brooke marries a stern clergyman (Mr. Casaubon) years older than herself in the hopes of helping him complete his great work of theology. The two travel to Rome for that purpose, but Dorothea finds her assistance unwanted. Along the way she runs into Casaubon's estranged cousin Will Ladislaw, a wandering artist with whom she strikes up a friendship. Just before the Casaubons leave Rome, Will comes to call.]

Will had not been invited to dine the next day. Hence he persuaded himself that he was bound to call, and that the only eligible time was the middle of the day, when Mr. Casaubon would not be at home.

Dorothea, who had not been made aware that her former reception of Will had displeased her husband, had no hesitation about seeing him, especially as he might be come to pay a farewell visit. When he entered she was looking at some cameos which she had been buying for Celia. She greeted Will as if his visit were quite a matter of course, and said at once, having a cameo bracelet in her hand—

"I am so glad you are come. Perhaps you understand all about cameos, and can tell me if these are really good. I wished to have you with us in choosing them, but Mr. Casaubon objected: he thought there was not time. He will finish his work to-morrow, and we shall go away in three days. I have been uneasy about these cameos. Pray sit down and look at them."

"I am not particularly knowing, but there can be no great mistake about these little Homeric bits: they are exquisitely neat. And the color is fine: it will just suit you."

"Oh, they are for my sister, who has quite a different complexion. You saw her with me at Lowick: she is light-haired and very pretty— at least I think so. We were never so long away from each other in our lives before. She is a great pet and never was naughty in her life. I found out before I came away that she wanted me to buy her some cameos, and I should be sorry for them not to be good—after their kind." Dorothea added the last words with a smile.

"You seem not to care about cameos," said Will, seating himself at some distance from her, and observing her while she closed the cases.

"No, frankly, I don't think them a great object in life," said Dorothea

"I fear you are a heretic about art generally. How is that? I should have expected you to be very sensitive to the beautiful everywhere."

"I suppose I am dull about many things," said Dorothea, simply. "I should like to make life beautiful—I mean everybody's life. And then all this immense expense of art, that seems somehow to lie outside life and make it no better for the world, pains one. It spoils my enjoyment of anything when I am made to think that most people are shut out from it."

"I call that the fanaticism of sympathy," said Will, impetuously. "You might say the same of landscape, of poetry, of all refinement. If you carried it out you ought to be miserable in your own goodness, and turn evil that you might have no advantage over others. The best piety is to enjoy—when you can. You are doing the most then to save the earth's character as an agreeable planet. And enjoyment radiates. It is of no use to try and take care of all the world; that is being taken care of when you feel delight—in art or in anything else. Would you turn all the youth of the world into a tragic chorus, wailing and moralizing over misery? I suspect that you have some false belief in the virtues of misery, and want to make your life a martyrdom." Will had gone further than he intended, and checked himself. But Dorothea's thought was not taking just the same direction as his own, and she answered without any special emotion—

"Indeed you mistake me. I am not a sad, melancholy creature. I am never unhappy long together. I am angry and naughty—not like Celia: I have a great outburst, and then all seems glorious again. I cannot help believing in glorious things in a blind sort of way. I should be quite willing to enjoy the art here, but there is so much that I don't know the reason of—so much that seems to me a consecration of ugliness rather than beauty. The painting and sculpture may be wonderful, but the feeling is often low and brutal, and sometimes even ridiculous. Here and there I see what takes me at once as noble—something that I might compare with the Alban Mountains or the sunset from the Pincian Hill; but that makes it the greater pity that there is so little of the best kind among all that mass of things over which men have toiled so."

"Of course there is always a great deal of poor work: the rarer things want that soil to grow in."

"Oh dear," said Dorothea, taking up that thought into the chief current of her anxiety; "I see it must be very difficult to do anything good. I have often felt since I have been in Rome that most of our lives would look much uglier and more bungling than the pictures, if they could be put on the wall."

# EASTERTIDE WEEK 4

## *Watch for the Sun*

### OPENING PRAYER

I cannot see, my God, a reason why
From morn to night I go not gladsome, free;
For, if thou art what my soul thinketh thee,
There is no burden but should lightly lie,
No duty but a joy at heart must be:
Love's perfect will can be nor sore nor small,
For God is light—in him no darkness is at all.
— George MacDonald (Scottish, 1824–1905)

### SCRIPTURES

Psalm 130 | Lamentations 3:21–33 | Romans 13:11–14 |
Mark 16:9–20

### READINGS

"Unquiet Vigil" by Brother Paul Quenon
"To His Sweet Savior" by Robert Herrick
"Helping the Morning" by Jeanne Murray Walker
"Experience bows a sweet contented face" by Christina Rossetti
"Miracle in the Garden" by Benjamín Alire Sáenz
"Prayer" by Augustine of Hippo, adapted by Scott Cairns
From *Parables from Nature: Waiting* by Margaret Gatty

### PERSONAL PRAYER AND REFLECTION

CLOSING PRAYER

O Master, my desires to work, to know,
To be aware that I do live and grow—
All restless wish for anything not thee,
I yield, and on thy altar offer me.
Let me no more from out thy presence go,
But keep me waiting watchful for thy will—
Even while I do it, waiting watchful still.
— GEORGE MACDONALD (Scottish, 1824–1905)

# READINGS

## Unquiet Vigil
BROTHER PAUL QUENON (Anglo-American, contemporary)

Stale prayer from
unreal depths—
depths I assume are mine—

are relieved by
real sleep,
that awakens me to my

real shallows where
prayer amounts to
almost nothing
or less.

Such an infinity where
almost nothing
dividing endlessly
never reaches
nothing

wherein are
real depths
not mine …

Be kind.
Myself, to myself, be kind.

———

## To His Sweet Savior
ROBERT HERRICK (English, 1591–1674)

Night hath no wings to him that cannot sleep,
And time seems then not for to fly, but creep;
Slowly her chariot drives, as if that she
Had broke her wheel, or crack'd her axletree.
Just so it is with me, who, list'ning, pray
The winds to blow the tedious night away,
That I might see the cheerful, peeping day.
Sick is my heart! O Savior! do Thou please
To make my bed soft in my sicknesses:
Lighten my candle, so that I beneath
Sleep not for ever in the vaults of death;
Let me Thy voice betimes i' th' morning hear:
Call, and I'll come; say Thou the when, and where.
Draw me but first, and after Thee I'll run
And make no one stop till my race be done.

———

## Helping the Morning
JEANNE MURRAY WALKER (Anglo-American, contemporary)

After the graveside, after the ride home, after
    a winter of drought, the chain
        and padlock on my heart,

morning shows up at my bedside,
    almost too late, like a big sister
        holding a glass of water

and I drink, glancing through the window
    at the tiny red barn flung
        into the lap of the brown valley below.

I am amazed at the silent, terrible wonder
    of my health. I am giddy at the lack of war.
        I want to help the morning.

I pray the bedpost, the windowpanes.
    I put our children on two doorknobs,
        Our sick friends in mirrors.

Like the aperture of a camera, the morning opens
    and keeps opening until the room is filled
        with rosy light and I could believe

anything: that grass might turn green again,
    that cloud the size of my hand
        might swell, might drift in, bringing rain.

———

## 'Experience bows a sweet contented face'
CHRISTINA ROSSETTI (English, 1830–1894)

Experience bows a sweet contented face.
　　Still setting to her seal that God is true:
　　Beneath the sun, she knows, is nothing new;
All things that go return with measured pace,
Winds, rivers, man's still recommencing race: —
　　While Hope beyond earth's circle strains her view.
　　Past sun and moon, and rain and rainbow too,
Enamored of unseen eternal grace.
Experience saith, 'My God doth all things well':
　　And for the morrow taketh little care,
　　　Such peace and patience garrison her soul: —
　　　While Hope, who never yet hath eyed the goal,
　　With arms flung forth, and backward-floating hair.
Touches, embraces, hugs the invisible.

———

## Miracle in the Garden
BENJAMÍN ALIRE SÁENZ (Mexican-American, contemporary)

　　　*"I have seen the Lord."*
　　　—John 20:18

You gave and gave, but it was not enough.
And there you were again—alone.
Another loss. Another wound. Another
scar: on the skin, in the heart, on the face.
The body wears the pain. Those hurts
come back—again—those hurts—again—
childhood and old lovers come back
always: they rise like Lazarus

needing no Jesus to command them back
to life. Overcome with grief—
more tears? So many droughts
and still more water in the well?
I sat across from you—in your garden—Spring—
and the sun shining like a new flower in bloom
haloing    you    me    the entire garden. You
did not notice the warmth. I was silent
in the presence of your grief. I was
there to pay respects, but not to speak.
In the sunlight, as I watched,
I had the urge to dip my hand
in the water of your tears,
and pray and bless myself
in the name of all your pain.

For a time, you walked that bridge
between the present and the past, between
this world and the next—*would it be better there?*
Your eyes stared blank—far—you
wanted to go, no longer wanting to choose
life. You sobbed out your regrets,
shook and shook your head. You clenched
your jaw as if to say: *I'll never love again,*
*I'll never love.* You grew quiet
listening to your god, or to your heart,
or to the western sun lighting up
the earth—the sun that set and rose,
the ceaseless sun that never tired
of the job that it was given. You felt
its labor on your skin. You were warmed—and then you
laughed. I saw you rising then. I saw you rise.

———

## Prayer

AUGUSTINE OF HIPPO (North African, ca. 354–430)
adapted by Scott Cairns

Here and now—why not?—let
there rise—even as You
provide it, even as You grant
both pleasure and ability—let
there spring, at long last, truth
from the earth, and let joy
in finally *doing* something
settle on us from heaven.

Yes, we have thought good
thoughts, and guessed
good thoughts were plenty.
High time for a little light
in the firmament. High time
we did as we thought, did
as we said. Help us.
And look! New fruit
leaps from the earth,
and this because the earth
is good. May we see
our momentary light
burst forth and—born
of good work and the sweet
savor of contemplation, born
of the Word of Life above—
let us appear as sudden lights,
drawing radiance from the lush
firmament of Your Scripture.

From *Parables from Nature: Waiting*
MARGARET GATTY (English, 1809–1873)

> *"It is good that a man should both hope and quietly wait."*
> —Lamentations 3:6

It was, doubtless, a very sorry life the House Cricket led, before houses were built and fires were kindled. There was no comfortable kitchen-hearth then, in the warm nooks and corners of which he might sit and sing his cheerful song, coming out every now and then to bask himself in the glow of the blazing light. On the contrary, he, so fond of heat, had no place to shelter in but holes in hollow trees, or crevices in rocks and stones, or some equally dull and damp abode. Besides which, he had to bear the incessant taunts and ridicule of creatures who were perfectly comfortable themselves, and so had no fellow-feeling for his want of cheerfulness.

"Why don't you go and spring about, and sing in the fields with your cousin, the Grasshopper?" was the ill-natured question of the Spider, as she twisted her web in one of the refuge-holes the Cricket had crept into; "I am sure your legs are long enough, if you would only take the trouble to undouble them. It's nothing but a sulky, discontented feeling that keeps you and all your family moping in these out-of-the-way corners, when you ought to be using your limbs in jumping about and enjoying yourself. And I dare say, too, that you could sing a great deal louder if you chose."

The Cricket thought perhaps he could—but he must feel very differently to what he did then, before it would be possible to try. Something was so very very wrong with him, but what that something was he did not know. All the other beasts and birds and insects seemed easy and happy enough. The Spider, for instance, was quite at home and gay in the hole *he* found so dismal.

And it was not the Spider only who was contented: the Flies—the Bees—the Ants—the very Mole, who sometimes came up from burrowing, and told wonderful stories of his underground delights—the birds with their merry songs—the huge beasts, who walked about like giants in the fields—all—all were satisfied with their condition, and happy in themselves. Every one had the home he liked, and no one envied the other.

But with him it was quite otherwise: he never felt at home! on the contrary, it always seemed to him that he was looking out for something that was not there, some place that could never be found, some state where he could rise out of the depression and uneasiness which here seemed to clog him down, though he could not understand why.

Poor fellow! as things were now, he felt for ever driven to hide in holes, although he knew that his limbs were built for energy; and few ever heard his voice, though he possessed one fitted for something much better than doleful complaints…

…Oh, this yearning after some other better state that lies unrevealed in the indefinite future—how restless and disheartening a sensation! Oh, this painful contrast of perfection in all created things around, to the lonely meditator on so much happiness, who is the solitary exception to the rule—how trying the position! How cruel, how almost overwhelming the struggle between the iron chain of reality and the soaring wing of aspiration!

But, "What is the use, my poor good friends," expostulated a plodding old Mole one day, after coming out to see how the upper world went on, and hearing the Cricket's complaints—"what is the use of all this groaning and conjecturing? You admit that every other creature but yourself is perfect in its way, and quite happy. Well, then, I will tell you that you ought to be quite sure you are perfect in your way too, though you have not found it out yet; and that you will be happy one day or other, although it may not be the case just now. Do you suppose this fine scheme of things we live in is to be soiled with one speck of dirt, as it were for the sake of teasing such a little insignificant creature as yourself! Don't think it for a moment, for it is not at all likely! But you must not suppose that everything goes right at first even with the best of us. I have had some small experience, and I know. But everything fits in at last. Of that I am quite sure. For instance, now, I do not suppose it ever occurred to you to think what a trial it must be to a young Mole when he first begins to burrow in the earth. Do you imagine that he knows what he is doing it for, or what will be the result? No such thing. It is a complete working in the dark, not knowing in the least where he is going. Dear me! if one had once stopped to conjecture and puzzle, what a hardship it would have seemed to drive one's nose by the hour together into unknown ground, for some unexplained reason that did not come out for some time afterwards, and that one had no certainty would ever come out at all! But everything fits in at last. And so it did with us. I remember it quite well in my own case. We drove the earth away and outwards, till the space so cleared proved an absolute palace! By the bye, I must try and get you down into our splendid abode—it will cheer you up, and teach you a useful lesson. Well, so you see we found out at last what all the grubbing had been for—"

"—Ah! but," interrupted the Cricket, "you were laboring for *some* purpose all the time, and if I had to labor I could hope. The difficulty is, to sit moping with nothing to do but *wait*."

"It is nonsense to talk of nothing to do," answered the Mole; "every creature has *something* to do. You, for instance, have always to watch for the sun. You know you like the beams and warmth he sends out better than anything else in the world, so you should get into the way of them as much as you can. And after the sun has set, you must hunt up the snuggest holes you can find, and so make the best of things as they are; and for the rest, you must *wait*. And waiting answers sometimes as well as working, I can assure you. There was the young Ox in the plains near here. As soon as he could run about at all, he began driving his clumsy head against everything he met. No one could tell why; but he fidgeted and butted about all day long, and many of his friends and acquaintances were very much offended by his manners. Others laughed. The dogs, indeed, were particularly amused, and used to bark at him constantly—even close to his nose sometimes, as he lowered his head after them. Well, at last, out came the secret. Two fine horns grew out from our friend's head, and people soon understood the meaning of all the butting; and one of the saucy curs who was playing the old barking game with him one day got finely tossed for his pains. Everything fits in at last, my friends! No cravings are given in vain. There is always something in store to account for them, you may be quite sure. You *may* have to wait a bit—some of you a shorter, some a longer time; but *do* wait—and everything will fit in and be perfect at last." . . .

. . . It was a most fortunate circumstance for the Crickets that the Mole happened to give them this good advice; for a malicious Ape had lately been suggesting to them, whether, as they were totally useless and very unhappy, it would not be a good thing for them all, to starve themselves to death, or in some other way, to rid the world of their whole race.

But the Mole's good sense gave a different turn to their ideas; and hope is so natural and pleasant a feeling, that when once they ventured to encourage it, it flourished and grew in their hearts till it created a sort of happiness of itself. In short, they determined to *wait* and meantime to watch for the sun, as their friend had advised. . . .

. . . But, truly, though it tarried, the day of deliverance and joy did come! The first fire that ever warmed the hearthstone that flagged the grand old chimney-arch of ancient times, ended for ever the mystery of the House Crickets' wants and cravings; and when it commonly blazed every winter night in men's dwellings, all the doubts and woes of Cricket life were over...These seemed to have passed away like the dreams of a disturbed night, which had been succeeded by daylight and reality. And oh, what ecstasy of joy the Crickets felt! How loud they shouted, and how high they sprang! "We knew it would be so! The good old Mole was right! The grumbling beasts were wrong! Everything is perfect now, and no one is so happy as we are."

"Grandmother, what creature is it that I hear singing so loudly in the corner by the fire?" inquires the little one of the good old dame who sits musing on the oaken settle.

"I do not hear it, my child, and I do not know," answers the deaf and blind old crone. "But if it be singing, love, it is happy, and enjoys these blessed fires as much as I do. 'Let everything that hath breath praise the Lord.'"

Ah! it was no wonder that amidst the many merry voices that then shouted, and still shout, round those warm and friendly fires, no voice is louder, no joy more grateful, than that of the patient Cricket. . . .

## EASTERTIDE WEEK 5

# Companions in the Light

OPENING PRAYER

lord
when you arrive
we'll be light
bread and water
the table is set and the door ajar
come and be seated among us
free me of the belief
that you're only faithful from a distance
and speak with me
in the unhurried speech of animals
who watch us from afar
with their unadulterated hunger
—SAID (Iranian, contemporary)

SCRIPTURES

PSALM 27 | MICAH 4:1–7 | ROMANS 8:18–27 | LUKE 24:36–53

READINGS

"A Night Visitor" by BROTHER PAUL QUENON
"The Dawning" by GEORGE HERBERT
Hymn based on St. Patrick's Breastplate (also known as "The Deer's
Cry") by PATRICK OF IRELAND
"Miserere" by MARGARET PHILBRICK
From *Death Comes for the Deconstructionist* by DANIEL TAYLOR

PERSONAL PRAYER AND REFLECTION

CLOSING PRAYER

Thou near then, I draw nearer—to thy feet,
And sitting in thy shadow, look out on the shine;
Ready at thy first word to leave my seat—
Not thee: thou goest too. From every clod
Into thy footprint flows the indwelling wine;
And in my daily bread, keen-eyed I greet
Its being's heart, the very body of God.
—GEORGE MACDONALD (Scottish, 1824–1905)

# READINGS

## *A Night Visitor*
BROTHER PAUL QUENON (Anglo-American, contemporary)

A grey cloud cover
hides the moon, blanketing light
as night grows lonely.

My ears are stifled
by the crush of my own thoughts
'til silence says: Hush.

These ears are windows
Opening on quiet night
where my soul can breathe.

If I could reach out
to touch this fragile silence
she would shy away.

She offers presence,
not familiarity,
to my calloused hand.

Close as my own breath,
though my mind be far away,
precious as a prayer.

Rare is the moment
when, with nothing on my mind,
I hear her passage,

subtle as a sigh.

———

## The Dawning
GEORGE HERBERT (English, 1593–1633)

Awake sad heart, whom sorrow ever drowns;
    Take up thine eyes, which feed on earth;
Unfold thy forehead, gathered into frowns;
    Thy Savior comes, and with Him mirth:
                Awake, awake,
And with a thankful heart His comforts take.
      But thou dost still lament, and pine, and cry,
      And feel His death, but not His victory.

Arise sad heart; if thou dost not withstand,
    Christ's resurrection thine may be;
Do not by hanging down break from the hand
    Which, as it riseth, raiseth thee:
                Arise, arise,
And with His burial-linen dry thine eyes.
      Christ left His grave-clothes, that we might, when grief
      Draws tears or blood, not want an handkerchief.

———

## Hymn based on St. Patrick's Breastplate (also known as "The Deer's Cry")

PATRICK OF IRELAND (Irish, ca. 387–461)

I bind unto myself today
The strong Name of the Trinity
By invocation of the same,
The Three in One, and One in Three.

I bind this day to me forever,
By power of faith, Christ's Incarnation;
His baptism in the Jordan river;
His death on the cross for my salvation.
His bursting from the spiced tomb;
His riding up the heav'nly way;
His coming at the day of doom:
I bind unto myself today.

I bind unto myself the power
Of the great love of cherubim;
The sweet "Well done" in judgment hour;
The service of the seraphim:
Confessors' faith, apostle's word,
The patriarch's prayers, the prophet's scrolls;
All good deeds done unto the Lord,
And purity of virgin souls.

I bind unto myself today
The virtues of the starlit heav'n,
The glorious sun's life-giving ray,
The whiteness of the moon at even,
The flashing of the lightning free,
The whirling wind's tempestuous shocks,
The stable earth, the deep salt sea,
Around the old eternal rocks.

I bind unto myself today
The power of God to hold and lead,
His eye to watch, his might to stay,
His ear to hearken to my need;
The wisdom of my God to teach,
His hand to guide, his shield to ward;
The word of God to give me speech,
His heav'nly host to be my guard.

Christ be with me, Christ within me,
Christ behind me, Christ before me,
Christ beside me, Christ to win me,
Christ to comfort and restore me,
Christ beneath me, Christ above me,
Christ in quiet, Christ in danger,
Christ in hearts of all that love me,
Christ in mouth of friend and stranger.

I bind unto myself the Name,
The strong Name of the Trinity;
By invocation of the same,
The Three in One, and One in Three.
Of whom all nature hath creation;
Eternal Father, Spirit, Word;
Praise to the Lord of my salvation,
Salvation is of Christ the Lord.

Amen.

————

## *Miserere*
MARGARET PHILBRICK (Anglo-American, contemporary)

Sunsets blue on San Miniato al Monte,
keeping time with Vesper monks,
chanting Latin in dusty robes as
yellow warmth stripes the ancient floor.
Kneelers creek,
knees rub,
prayers rise
with incense, harmonies unseen.
Sunlight bridges an ocean of years,
antiphonal groanings now in street clothes.
Scuffed shoes ascend, descend
modernist steps and answer
the hunger of hearts for echo,
of cries unceasing,
hearts unending.
Linking us with the holy,
with the solely, devoted
suffering servants
of His choir.

———

## FROM *Death Comes for the Deconstructionist*
DANIEL TAYLOR (Anglo-American, contemporary)

[Editor's note: When the famous literary theorist, Professor Richard Pratt, turns up dead after a public lecture, his widow calls upon
his former graduate student (and dropout), Jon Mote, our narrator.
Jon, along with his mentally impaired sister, Judy—one of the most
endearing sidekicks in all of detective fiction—set out to solve the
mystery. Something is definitely amiss, but we begin to realize that

without Judy to intercede, it's Jon's own soul that's in danger of being deconstructed.]

I feel sick the rest of the week—all weakness and flight. I can tell Judy is worried about me. Normally she treats me with the benign superiority of a big sister. But when she is worried, she starts to hover. She especially doesn't like me going to bed in the daytime, no matter how lousy I feel.

Judy watches as I lie down on the couch for the third time in two days.

"I . . . I do not think, Jon, that you should be . . . I should say . . . that you should be sleeping so much. Sister Brigit says it . . . it is not good for you."

"Sister Brigit is way too anal."

Judy just looks at me with a few solemn blinks. I feel guilty, my default stance toward life.

"Listen, Jude. I don't feel well, see? It's that simple. When people feel crummy they lie down. It's not a crime against God or man or Sister Brigit. Do I have to accomplish something every lousy day of my lousy life? Can't I just be? Can't I sometimes buy a pound of hamburger with my good looks? Huh? Why become a worker ant serving the Queen Bee of Productivity? Jeez, Jude, I had a wife once. I don't need the spirit of Sister Brigit hanging over me. I just want to get up some morning and feel that the universe approves of me just for existing. Just for breathing in and out. You know, just how Margaret Mead reported those Pacific Islanders feel. Accepting life and themselves and sex. If you're hungry, just reach out for that mango hanging above your head. If you're horny, just smile naturally at the next naturally good-looking girl that sarongs naturally by. Were they pulling her leg? Could it have been that easy—that guiltless? Why doesn't it ever work north of the equator? Is it the water? Is love—or anything else—ever really free? Will any woman anywhere ever be genuinely indifferent when she sees her lover making eyes at someone else? It's hard to believe, Jude. I mean it's really hard to believe. I've been asked to swallow whoppers all my life. First it was Bible whoppers—granddaddy creator, water turned to blood, chariots of fire, the dead come back to life. Then it was science whoppers—Big Bang plus time equals me. Out of dead matter . . . life! Out of chemicals . . . Consciousness! At least with the big Bible whoppers there was an equally big payoff—glory by and by, everything evened up and everybody happy . . . maybe the biggest whopper of them all. I mean everybody happy, Jude? No pain? No suffering? No stomachaches? You don't got to be no Sigmund I. M. Freud to see that's wishing more than thinking. But how am I any better off for not believing it? Why is that any more of a stretch than sea water plus lightning, bake for a few billion years, and you get the Sistine Chapel…or Michael Jordan going to the basket? Whoppers! Whoppers all around!"

I wind down like a Christmas toy on a dying battery.

"Are . . . are you finished, Jon?"

"Yes, I'm finished." It isn't pleasant doing improv performance art in front of an unappreciative audience of one.

"I just . . . just want to say, Jon, that Jesus . . . I should say, Jesus loves you . . . very much."

Great, that and five bucks will get me coffee at Starbucks.

I just said I'm sick for the rest of the week, but to tell the truth I've never been very good at measuring out time. Maybe it's been a week, maybe not. Time does not so much pass for me as it escapes—even hides. When I lived with Uncle Lester, I would finish breakfast and next thing I knew I'd hear them calling me to supper. I would be sure it was Thursday, only to find it was Saturday. I'd be listening to the first inning of the baseball game on the radio and next thing I knew the game had been over for an hour.

Maybe that's why I've had trouble making a living since I quit getting free meals in the army. If time is money, I'm a pauper on both counts. Zillah used to say I lost track of time on purpose. After another of my famous no-shows, she said, "If you think losing track of time gets you off the hook, Jon, you've got another think coming."

I didn't know exactly what she meant, but then I often didn't know what Zillah meant, or if she even meant to mean anything. She was just frustrated living with a psychological black hole.

In my own defense, I don't think I get enough credit for accomplishing simple things. Zillah never realized how much effort I expend just getting myself upright in the morning. If life is a race, I'm running in cement boots, but at least I'm doing the work. From a certain point of view, I'm even courageous.

But it takes more than a certain point of view to make a woman happy. I know how Zillah felt. I wasn't happy living with him either.

Maybe that's why I missed Judy so much over the years. When we were kids she could keep me patched together. She could do what all the king's horses and all the king's men couldn't. It wasn't what she said. She never said anything she hadn't heard someone else already say. It was just, I don't know, her presence—maybe with a capital P. She has a quality of being that is somehow soothing. Maybe she lacks the complexity necessary for sustained unhappiness. She is elemental in a compound world.

I remember the time not too long after we went to live with Uncle Lester. I'd gotten a whipping for something. I don't remember exactly what—with Uncle Lester most any excuse for a whipping would do. Apparently I sort of went off the deep end this time. I guess I cursed him and kicked him in the shins, but I can't say I remember it. (I wish I did.) What I remember is finding myself in the closet with Judy sitting next to me talking. I remember us sitting on shoes and dark winter coats hanging down around our heads, my face hot and wet with tears.

"It will be . . . I should say . . . it will be all right, Jon. He is gone. He will . . . he will not hit you any . . . anymore. I am here with you my own self. Are you hearing . . . I should say . . . hearing me, Jon? You . . . you come back now."

Judy was forever saying things were going to be all right. She never offered a shred of evidence to back up such an outrageous claim. She never gave reasons or arguments or precedents or anything— just bald assertion. Everything is going to be "all right." My God, what unsupportable optimism! All right? All right? Everything in its place? Everything as it should be? What could ever lead anyone in this wasteland of a world to come to that conclusion? Shantih my ass.

And yet, I don't know, there is something persuasive about Judy. You know she can't read, add numbers, dial the telephone, or quite comprehend a calendar. But you also feel she was born knowing things the rest of us never quite learn. She came into this world trailing clouds of glory, and, somehow, avoided the prison house of adult perception. She projects trustworthiness. If she can't calculate, she also cannot be calculating. She cannot strategize, maneuver, orchestrate, simulate, feign, invent, hedge, or dissemble. She is therefore totally unfit for this world, or most fit of all. All I know is that when I lost her the first time, I lost my best hope. I can't afford to lose her again.

# EASTERTIDE WEEK 6

## *I Shall Live Forever!*

OPENING PRAYER

Thy grace, O Father, give,
I humbly thee implore;
And let thy mercy bless
Thy servant more and more.
All grace and glory be to thee
From age to age eternally.
—GREGORY OF NAZIANZUS (Cappadocia/
modern-day Turkey, AD 325–390)

SCRIPTURES

PSALM 112 | EZEKIEL 36:22–28 | 1 CORINTHIANS 15:50–57 |
JOHN 21:20–25

READINGS

From "Sabbaths 2006 (VII)" by WENDELL BERRY
"No coward soul is mine" by EMILY BRONTË
"My Silence Is the Lord" by BROTHER PAUL QUENON
"Death be not proud (Divine Meditations: X)" by JOHN DONNE
"Evening Promise" by PAUL J. WILLIS
From *The Secret Garden* by FRANCES HODGSON BURNETT

PERSONAL PRAYER AND REFLECTION

CLOSING PRAYER

. . . Cleansed from filthy stain,
I may meet[29] homage give,

And, pure in heart, behold
And serve thee while I live;
Clean hands in holy worship raise,
And thee, O Christ my Savior, praise.
—GREGORY OF NAZIANZUS (Cappadocia/
modern-day Turkey, AD 325–390)

# READINGS

## FROM *Sabbaths 2006 (VII)*
WENDELL BERRY (Anglo-American, contemporary)

O saints, if I am even eligible for this prayer,
though less than worthy of this dear desire,
and if your prayers have influence in Heaven,
let my place there be lower than your own.
I know how you longed, here where you lived
as exiles, for the presence of the essential
Being and Maker and Knower of all things.
But because of my unruliness, or some erring
virtue in me never rightly schooled,
some error clear and dear, my life
has not taught me your desire for flight:
dismattered, pure, and free. I long
instead for the Heaven of creatures, of seasons,
of day and night. Heaven enough for me
would be this world as I know it, but redeemed
of our abuse of it and one another. It would be
the Heaven of knowing again. There is no marrying
in Heaven, and I submit: even so, I would like
to know my wife again, both of us young again,
and I remembering always how I loved her

when she was old. I would like to know
my children again, all my family, all my dear ones,
to see, to hear, to hold, more carefully
than before, to study them lingeringly as one
studies old verses, committing them to heart
forever. I would like again to know my friends,
my old companions, men and women, horses
and dogs, in all the ages of our lives, here
in this place that I have watched over all my life
in all its moods and seasons, never enough.
I will be leaving how many beauties overlooked?
A painful Heaven this would be, for I would know
by it how far I have fallen short. I have not
paid enough attention, I have not been grateful
enough. And yet this pain would be the measure
of my love. In eternity's once and now, pain would
place me surely in the Heaven of my earthly love.

———

## 'No coward soul is mine'
EMILY BRONTË (English, 1818–1848)

No coward soul is mine,
No trembler in the world's storm-troubled sphere:
I see Heaven's glories shine,
And faith shines equal, arming me from fear.

O God within my breast,
Almighty, ever-present Deity!
Life—that in me has rest,
As I—undying Life—have Power in Thee!

Vain are the thousand creeds
That move men's hearts: unutterably vain;
Worthless as withered weeds,
Or idlest froth amid the boundless main,

To waken doubt in one
Holding so fast by thine infinity;
So surely anchored on
The steadfast rock of immortality.

With wide-embracing love
Thy spirit animates eternal years,
Pervades and broods above,
Changes, sustains, dissolves, creates, and rears.

Though earth and man were gone,
And suns and universes ceased to be,
And Thou wert left alone,
Every existence would exist in Thee.

There is not room for Death,
Nor atom that his might could render void:
Thou—Thou art Being and Breath,
And what Thou art may never be destroyed.

———

## My Silence Is the Lord
BROTHER PAUL QUENON (Anglo-American, contemporary)

My silence is the Lord,
I listen, his silence speaks at all times.
When I listen not, my hearing is filled with words
and my tongue takes to rambling.

My resting place is the Lord
a hideaway on a mountain height.
The lonely seek and find him.

My resting place is the Lord,
a low valley by the runlet.
All humble steps lead there.

"Turn in to my place and sit quietly.
Drink from my stream and my vintage.
Cast off your shoes, discard your hardships
and listen to my evening song:

"I seek a heart that is simple.
With the peaceful I spread my tent.
I will wash your feet and dry them,
my silence will be their perfume.

"In your quiet steps I will follow.
None will know whence we come and where we go.
To the world you will be my silence,
in your passing they will hear me.

"In your absence I will be present.
Though you die, I Who Live am yours—
I live as yours forever."

———

## 'Death be not proud' (Divine Meditations: X)
JOHN DONNE (English, 1572–1631)

Death be not proud, though some have called thee
Mighty and dreadful, for, thou art not so,
For, those, whom thou think'st, thou dost overthrow,
Die not, poor death, nor yet canst thou kill me.

From rest and sleep, which but thy pictures be,
Much pleasure, then from thee, much more must flow,
And soonest our best men with thee do go,
Rest of their bones, and soul's delivery.
Thou art slave to fate, chance, kings, and desperate men,
And dost with poison, war, and sickness dwell,
And poppy, or charms can make us sleep as well,
And better than thy stroke; why swell'st thou then?
One short sleep past, we wake eternally,
And death shall be no more; death, thou shalt die.

————

## Evening Promise
PAUL J. WILLIS (Anglo-American, contemporary)

*for Hanna*

When you wake
you will know that stars fade
that night does not last
that the sorrows of planets
are the joys of morning
that birds repair and lemons kindle
out your window
nature's first lesson
first hint
of grace.

————

## From *The Secret Garden*
FRANCES HODGSON BURNETT (English-American, 1849–1924)

[Editor's note: As Mary Lennox's adventures continue at her uncle's manor, she discovers an abandoned secret garden and begins to clear it out with the help of old Ben Weatherstaff, the gardener, and a young boy named Dickon, who seems to embody the spirit of the good earth itself. Dickon and Mary bring Colin to the garden day by day; and as spring progresses, Colin grows stronger: he not only abandons his wheelchair but begins to put on weight and to work the earth.]

It was not very long after [Colin] had said this that he laid down his trowel and stood up on his feet. He had been silent for several minutes and they had seen that he was thinking out lectures, as he often did. When he dropped his trowel and stood upright it seemed to Mary and Dickon as if a sudden strong thought had made him do it. He stretched himself out to his tallest height and he threw out his arms exultantly. Color glowed in his face and his strange eyes widened with joyfulness. All at once he had realized something to the full.

"Mary! Dickon!" he cried. "Just look at me!"

They stopped their weeding and looked at him.

"Do you remember that first morning you brought me in here?" he demanded.

Dickon was looking at him very hard. Being an animal charmer he could see more things than most people could and many of them were things he never talked about. He saw some of them now in this boy.

"Aye, that we do," he answered.

Mary looked hard too, but she said nothing.

"Just this minute," said Colin, "all at once I remembered it myself—when I looked at my hand digging with the trowel—and I had to stand up on my feet to see if it was real. And it *is* real! I'm *well*—I'm *well!*"

"Aye, that tha' art!" said Dickon.

"I'm well! I'm well!" said Colin again, and his face went quite red all over.

He had known it before in a way, he had hoped it and felt it and thought about it, but just at that minute something had rushed all through him—a sort of rapturous belief and realization and it had been so strong that he could not help calling out.

"I shall live forever and ever and ever!" he cried grandly. "I shall find out thousands and thousands of things. I shall find out about people and creatures and everything that grows—like Dickon—and I shall never stop making Magic. I'm well! I'm well! I feel—I feel as if I want to shout out something—something thankful, joyful!"

Ben Weatherstaff, who had been working near a rose-bush, glanced round at him.

"Tha' might sing th' Doxology," he suggested in his dryest grunt. He had no opinion of the Doxology and he did not make the suggestion with any particular reverence.

But Colin was of an exploring mind and he knew nothing about the Doxology.

"What is that?" he inquired.

"Dickon can sing it for thee, I'll warrant," replied Ben Weatherstaff.

Dickon answered with his all-perceiving animal charmer's smile.

"They sing it i' church," he said. "Mother says she believes th' skylarks sings it when they gets up i' th' mornin'."

"If she says that, it must be a nice song," Colin answered. "I've never been in a church myself. I was always too ill. Sing it, Dickon. I want to hear it."

Dickon was quite simple and unaffected about it. He understood what Colin felt better than Colin did himself. He understood by a sort of instinct so natural that he did not know it was understanding. He pulled off his cap and looked round still smiling.

"Tha' must take off tha' cap," he said to Colin, "an' so mun tha', Ben—an' tha' mun stand up, tha' knows."

Colin took off his cap and the sun shone on and warmed his thick hair as he watched Dickon intently. Ben Weatherstaff scrambled up from his knees and bared his head too with a sort of puzzled half-resentful look on his old face as if he didn't know exactly why he was doing this remarkable thing.

Dickon stood out among the trees and rose-bushes and began to sing in quite a simple matter-of-fact way and in a nice strong boy voice:

"Praise God from whom all blessings flow,

Praise Him all creatures here below,

Praise Him above ye Heavenly Host,

Praise Father, Son, and Holy Ghost.

Amen."

When he had finished, Ben Weatherstaff was standing quite still with his jaws set obstinately but with a disturbed look in his eyes fixed on Colin. Colin's face was thoughtful and appreciative.

"It is a very nice song," he said. "I like it. Perhaps it means just what I mean when I want to shout out that I am thankful to the Magic." He stopped and thought in a puzzled way. "Perhaps they are both the same thing. How can we know the exact names of everything? Sing it again, Dickon. Let us try, Mary. I want to sing it, too. It's my song. How does it begin? 'Praise God from whom all blessings flow'?"

And they sang it again, and Mary and Colin lifted their voices as musically as they could and Dickon's swelled quite loud and beautiful—and at the second line Ben Weatherstaff raspingly cleared his throat and at the third he joined in with such vigor that it seemed almost savage and when the "Amen" came to an end Mary observed that the very same thing had happened to him which had happened when he found out that Colin was not a cripple—his chin was twitching and he was staring and winking and his leathery old cheeks were wet.

"I never seed no sense in th' Doxology afore," he said hoarsely, "but I may change my mind i' time. I should say tha'd gone up five pound this week, Mester Colin—five on 'em!"

## Into God's Rest

### OPENING PRAYER

O Father, thou art my eternity.
Not on the clasp of consciousness—on thee
My life depends; and I can well afford
All to forget, so thou remember, Lord.
In thee I rest; in sleep thou dost me fold;
In thee I labor; still in thee, grow old;
And dying, shall I not in thee, my Life, be bold?
—GEORGE MACDONALD (Scottish, 1824–1905)

### SCRIPTURES

PSALM 37 | EZEKIEL 36:8–12 | HEBREWS 4:1–11 | MATTHEW 28:16–20

### READINGS

"How to Prepare for the Second Coming" by ABIGAIL CARROLL
"This is my play's last scene (Divine Meditations: VI)" by JOHN DONNE
"Sustainability" by PAUL J. WILLIS
"What good shall my life do me?" by CHRISTINA ROSSETTI
From *A Tale of Two Cities* by CHARLES DICKENS
From *Brendan* by FREDERICK BUECHNER
"Finite and Infinite" by ELIZABETH BARRETT BROWNING

### PERSONAL PRAYER AND REFLECTION

### CLOSING PRAYER

Most Holy God, into Whose Hands
I was born, Beloved of my soul, to whom

I have offered my consecrated flesh
since even my earliest days, entrust me
to a luminous angel, who will lift
my hand to guide me to the place
where I may drink, and rest, and gain
my strength in the embrace of my holy fathers.
—MACRINA THE YOUNGER (Turkish, ca. 327–379),
adapted by Scott Cairns

## READINGS

### How to Prepare for the Second Coming
ABIGAIL CARROLL (Anglo-American, contemporary)

Start by recalling the absolute goodness of rain
and repent for every grumble you have ever made
about the weather (this will take approximately

forever.) Next, you will want to commit a theft:
with deft lock-picking and a shrewd hand, steal
back the hours you fed to the hungry god of work,

then squander them on hydrangeas, Wordsworth,
voluntary sidewalk repair. Teach a child to lace
a shoe (your child or another's—any four-year-old

will do), and while you're at it, set the alarm
for three, and fumble through the dark to the pond
to guard the salamanders as they cross the road. If,

having accomplished these tasks, you wish
to go on, sit at your desk and carefully design
a few radical acts of grace, by which I mean

murder (of a sort): you must willfully, passionately
kill the living, breathing debt owed you by those
who stole your goods, your rights, or the jewel

that was the beating muscle of your hope. Apart
from this, you cannot know the full extent of love.
(For precedent, refer to the cross). Thrust

your nails into dirt and plant a few seeds (carrots,
radishes, perhaps); indeed, get scandalously intimate
with the earth. After all, it is where you will live

when the lamb lies down with the lion, and the lion
has become your friend. And when the water
of the new world breaks, all is said and done (heaven

and earth made one as the prophets foretold),
you will lose each doubt to a song—which is
a kind of praise—and reap the good you sowed.

———

## 'This is my play's last scene' (*Divine Meditations: VI*)
JOHN DONNE (English, 1572–1631)

This is my play's last scene, here heavens appoint
My pilgrimage's last mile; and my race
Idly, yet quickly run hath this last pace,
My span's last inch, my minute's latest point,
And gluttonous death, will instantly unjoint
My body, and soul, and I shall sleep a space,
But my'ever-waking part shall see that face,
Whose fear already shakes my every joint:
Then, as my soul, to heaven her first seat, takes flight,
And earth-borne body, in the earth shall dwell,

So, fall my sins, that all may have their right,
To where they are bred, and would press me, to hell.
Impute me righteous, thus purged of evil,
For thus I leave the world, the flesh, and devil.

———

## Sustainability

PAUL J. WILLIS (Anglo-American, contemporary)

(*Laryx lyallis*)

A few weeks after my mother died,
I dreamed that she was waiting for me
in a ravine of spring-green larches.
There was no worry in her eyes, and
she sat there with her knees drawn up,
content to be in the filtered sunlight.
Funny, because she never lived
among larch trees—my mom grew up
on an orange grove and raised us
in the Douglas fir. I do not live
among them either, apart from my rare
visits to the North Cascades. But when
I'm here, as now I am, sitting barefoot
on Cutthroat Pass among amber larches
bathing every bowl and basin,
I have a sense that she's okay,
and that I am too, born to witness what
I can within this green and golden world
which still persists, with or without us,
but mostly with us, I've come to believe.
Things and people pass away—
but that's when they become themselves.

There's a new heaven, a new earth,
around and about us—and not much
different from the better parts of the old.
We don't live there very often,
but when we do, eternity
ignites in a moment, light in the larches
that shines. And shines.

———

## "What good shall my life do me?"
CHRISTINA ROSSETTI (English, 1830–1894)

Have dead men long to wait?—

There is a certain term
For their bodies to the worm
And their souls at heaven gate.
Dust to dust, clod to clod,
These precious things of God,
Trampled underfoot by man
And beast the appointed years.—

Their longest life was but a span
For change and smiles and tears.
Is it worth while to live,
Rejoice and grieve,
Hope, fear, and die?
Man with man, truth with lie,
The slow show dwindles by:
At last what shall we have
Besides a grave?—

Lies and shows no more,
No fear, no pain,

But after hope and sleep
Dear joys again.
Those who sowed shall reap:
Those who bore
The Cross shall wear the Crown:
Those who clomb[30] the steep
There shall sit down.
The Shepherd of the sheep
Feeds His flock there,
In watered pastures fair
They rest and leap.
"Is it worth while to live?"
Be of good cheer:
Love casts out fear:
Rise up, achieve.

———

## From *A Tale of Two Cities*
CHARLES DICKENS (English, 1812–1870)

[Editor's note: The man who takes Charles Darnay's place at the Guillotine, Sydney Carton, is given a vision in which he glimpses the fates
of his enemies and friends—as well as what his sacrifice means for his
own soul: a life and lives redeemed.]

They said of him, about the city that night, that it was the peace-
fullest man's face ever beheld there. Many added that he looked
sublime and prophetic.

One of the most remarkable sufferers by the same axe—a
woman—had asked at the foot of the same scaffold, not long before,
to be allowed to write down the thoughts that were inspiring her.
If he had given any utterance to his, and they were prophetic, they
would have been these:

"I see Barsad, and Cly, Defarge, The Vengeance, the Juryman, the Judge, long ranks of the new oppressors who have risen on the destruction of the old, perishing by this retributive instrument, before it shall cease out of its present use. I see a beautiful city and a brilliant people rising from this abyss, and, in their struggles to be truly free, in their triumphs and defeats, through long years to come, I see the evil of this time and of the previous time of which this is the natural birth, gradually making expiation for itself and wearing out.

"I see the lives for which I lay down my life, peaceful, useful, prosperous and happy, in that England which I shall see no more. I see Her with a child upon her bosom, who bears my name. I see her father, aged and bent, but otherwise restored, and faithful to all men in his healing office, and at peace. I see the good old man, so long their friend, in ten years' time enriching them with all he has, and passing tranquilly to his reward.

"I see that I hold a sanctuary in their hearts, and in the hearts of their descendants, generations hence. I see her, an old woman, weeping for me on the anniversary of this day. I see her and her husband, their course done, lying side by side in their last earthly bed, and I know that each was not more honored and held sacred in the other's soul, than I was in the souls of both.

"I see that child who lay upon her bosom and who bore my name, a man winning his way up in that path of life which once was mine. I see him winning it so well, that my name is made illustrious there by the light of his. I see the blots I threw upon it, faded away. I see him, fore-most of just judges and honored men, bringing a boy of my name, with a forehead that I know and golden hair, to this place—then fair to look upon, with not a trace of this day's disfigurement—and I hear him tell the child my story, with a tender and a faltering voice.

"It is a far, far better thing that I do, than I have ever done; it is a far, far better rest that I go to than I have ever known."

From *Brendan*

FREDERICK BUECHNER (Anglo-American, contemporary)

[Editor's note: In *Brendan*'s closing pages, Finn tenderly recounts the end of the saint's stormy life.]

One winter sabbath he said mass for the nuns in the same church we built for them with a roof like the Cara's hull. You'd have thought he was aboard her indeed the way he wobbled about like he was walking a stormy deck. It took a nun under each arm to get him up again each time he kneeled. We was coming out the door afterwards when he told Briga he had to sit and rest. The snow was falling thick and we turned to help him back inside the church again. Before we could manage it he sunk down on the stone steps.

The nuns had filed out ahead of us hurrying along with their heads bent. They was most of them already dim as shadows in the flakes. A few of the last ones saw what had happened though. I remember them standing about at the foot of the stairs with their cloaks pulled close.

Briga was down on her knees by Brendan fussing over him. She took off her shawl and wrapped it about him. She pulled his cowl up over his head. He took his hands in hers and breathed on them. The snow itself was no whiter than his face. Already his beard was white.

"Pray for me, Brig," he said the best he could. "The tide's at the flow. I'm not half ready."

"You've nothing to fear, my dear," she said, "at all, at all." She was trying to keep the snow from his face with her hands spread.

"I fear going alone," he said. "The way is dark."

It was hard to catch his words over the wind. We was both of us bending close to hear.

"I fear the unknown of it," he said.

A pair of the nuns come up. They knelt on the step below us. They clasped their blue slender hands at their lips.

"I fear the presence of the King, Finn," he said. There was flakes in his lashes. "I fear the sentence of the judge."

Of all the words he'd spoken his whole life through those was the last. They was like the last hazels to fall from a laden branch or the last pitter-patter of a rain. His jaw didn't close after them till my hand closed it. It was Briga closed his eyes.

Briga and me and the two nuns carried him the rest of the way down the steps into the winter.

We buried him at Clonfert like he wanted, far from the sea.

Hugh, High King of Cashel, come to do him honor. The King of Connacht come as well and many small kings and cowlords, brehon lawmakers and druids.

Great and small alike, the whole land mourned him. Sailors call on his name in high winds to this day.

As to the sentence of the judge, I'm not one to know nor even if there be a judge at all. If I, Finn, was judge I'd know well enough though.

I'd sentence him to have mercy on himself. I'd sentence him less to strive for the glory of God than just to let it swell his sails if it can.

He said he feared going alone. If he has an ear to hear with yet, I'd tell him maybe he won't be alone at all. There's many in the Country of the Young will welcome him among them surely should there be such a country and the true Saint Patrick to ring him ashore with his bell.

Lest he ever think back on his old friend Finn and how I come to be so tangled in his life I never got round to living my own, I'd tell him maybe it was worth it even. I'd tell him he has my pardon anyhow.

Brendan, navigator, friend Bren, pray for us all then. Now and at the hour we're sentenced ourselves. Amen.

## Finite and Infinite

ELIZABETH BARRETT BROWNING (English, 1806–1861)

The wind sounds only in opposing straits,
The sea, beside the shore; man's spirit rends
Its quiet only up against the ends
Of wants and oppositions, loves and hates,
Where, worked and worn by passionate debates,
And losing by the loss it apprehends,
The flesh rocks round and every breath it sends
Is raveled to a sigh. All tortured states
Suppose a straitened place. Jehovah Lord,
Make room for rest, around me! out of sight
Now float me of the vexing land abhorred,
Till in deep calms of space my soul may right
Her nature, shoot large sail on lengthening cord,
And rush exultant on the Infinite.

# CLOSING THOUGHTS

See it? The sunrise? We've made it to the light of a new day. Christ has died; Christ is risen; and Christ will—like the dawn—come again. The promised Spirit of Pentecost is on its way; and in the company of bards and prophets, sinners and saints, we now bear witness to the already-not-yet kingdom in our midst. As Eastertide turns to Ordinary Time, as spring turns to summer, let us be, to paraphrase novelist Katherine Paterson, "spies for hope." May the readings that you've encountered here accompany you into the everlasting day.

Many of the following works were read or consulted during the creation of this anthology. Though not an exhaustive list, it offers a jumping-off point for deeper exploration of the themes prevalent during Lent, Holy Week, and Eastertide.

**Fiction**
- *A Ring of Endless Light* by Madeleine L'Engle
- *All Hallows' Eve* and *The Place of the Lion* by Charles Williams
- *Bridge to Terabithia* by Katherine Paterson
- *Death Comes for the Archbishop* by Willa Cather
- *Extremely Loud and Incredibly Close* by Jonathan Safran Foer
- *Housekeeping* by Marilynne Robinson
- *In the Garden of the North American Martyrs* by Tobias Wolff
- *Ironweed* by William Kennedy
- *Notes from Underground* by Fyodor Dostoevsky
- *The Bluest Eye* by Toni Morrison
- *The Chosen* by Chaim Potok
- *The Complete Fairy Tales* by George MacDonald
- *The Hour I First Believed* by Wally Lamb
- *The Lion, the Witch, and the Wardrobe* by C. S. Lewis
- *The Lord of the Rings* by J. R. R. Tolkien
- *The Man Born to Be King* by Dorothy Sayers
- *The Patron Saint of Liars* by Ann Patchett
- *The Poisonwood Bible* by Barbara Kingsolver
- *The Violent Bear it Away* and "A Good Man is Hard to Find" by Flannery O'Connor
- *The Wing* by Ray Buckley
- *Things Fall Apart* by Chinua Achebe

Poetry

- *Bent Upon Light* by Marjorie Stelmach
- *Beowulf* (author unknown)
- *Conspiracy of Light: Poems Inspired by the Legacy of C. S. Lewis* by D. S. Martin
- *New Collected Poems* by Wendell Berry
- *Practicing Silence: New and Selected Poems* by Bonnie Thurston
- *Recovered Body* by Scott Cairns
- *Remembering Jesus: Sonnets and Songs* by John Leax
- *Selected Poems* by W. H. Auden
- *Sinners Welcome* by Mary Karr
- *The Collected Poems of Langston Hughes*
- *The Complete Poems of Emily Dickinson*
- *The Complete Poems and Plays 1909-1950* by T. S. Eliot
- *The Complete Works of John Milton*
- *The Dirty Side of the Storm* by Martha Serpas
- *The Eyes The Window* by Marci Rae Johnson
- *The Sea Sleeps: New & Selected Poems* by Greg Miller
- *This Shadowy Place* by Dick Allen

## ACKNOWLEDGMENTS AND PERMISSIONS

The curation of this collection has been something of a blur, thanks in no small part to a pair of very busy little boys, ages two and five, to whom the previous anthologies were dedicated. If my sons turn out to be unliterary souls, it will not be for lack of exposure— and they certainly cannot blame their mother. We survived thanks to our amazing community at Sycamore Creek Church in Lansing, Michigan, which includes caregivers like Alice McKinstry and Tabitha Martin as well as writer-friends like Kristin Kratky and Erin Wasinger. Thanks also to my parents, Bob and Peg Faulman for hours, days, weeks of childcare; and most especially to my husband, Tom, who juggles pastoring said church and parenting said boys, and *still* manages to hide encouraging sticky-notes for his wife all over the house. My work and world is lighter because of you.

Special thanks also to the gracious publishers and literary centers that have gone out of their way to make their authors' works accessible for this anthology: in particular, *Christianity and Literature* journal (www.christianityandliterature.com); the Frederick Buechner Center (www.frederickbuechner.com); Paraclete Press (www.paracletepress. com); Wm. B. Eerdmans Publishing Company (www.eerdmans. com); Wipf and Stock Publishers (www.wipfandstock.com); and WordFarm (www.wordfarm.net).

*Acknowledgment is gratefully made for permission to include the following works or excerpts:*

ADICHIE, CHIMAMANDA NGOZI: excerpt from *Purple Hibiscus* (Algonquin Books of Chapel Hill, 2003). Copyright 2003 by Chimamanda Ngozi Adichie. Reprinted by permission of Algonquin Books of Chapel Hill. All rights reserved.

ADKINS, AMEY VICTORIA: "saturday." Reprinted with permission from *Divinity* magazine (Spring 2015), published by Duke University Divinity School.

ALLEN, L. N.: "Six Holy Week Triolets" used by permission of the author.

AUSTIN, DERRICK: "Byzantine Gold" first published in *Image* journal. "Vespers" first published in *OCHO*. Used by permission of the author.

BAUMGAERTNER, JILL PELÁEZ: selected poems from *What Cannot Be Fixed* (Cascade Books, an imprint of Wipf and Stock Publishers, 2014). Copyright 2014 by Jill Peláez Baumgaertner. Used by permission of Wipf and Stock Publishers.

BERRY, WENDELL: "Sabbaths 2006: VII" from *Imago Dei: Poems from Christianity and Literature*, ed. Jill Peláez Baumgaertner (Abilene Christian University Press, 2012). Used by permission of *Christianity and Literature*.

BUECHNER, FREDERICK: excerpts from *Brendan* (HarperSanFrancisco, an imprint of HarperCollins Publishers, 1987). Copyright 1987 by Frederick Buechner. Used by permission of Frederick Buechner Literary Assets, LLC.

BROWN, JERICHO: "1 Corinthians 13:11" from *The New Testament* (Copper Canyon Press, 2014). Copyright 2014 by Jericho Brown. Reprinted with the permission of The Permissions Company, Inc., on behalf of Copper Canyon Press, www. coppercanyon.org.

CAIRNS, SCOTT: "Evening Prayer" from *Compass of Affection: Poems New and Selected* (Paraclete Press, 2006). Copyright 2006 by Scott Cairns. Used by permission of Paraclete Press. Selected poems from *Endless Life: Poems of the Mystics* (Paraclete Press, 2007). Copyright 2007 by Scott Cairns. Used by permission of Paraclete Press.

Great Banquet" published in *The Curator* journal and in *Basic Disaster Supplies Kit*. All poems, including "Easter Service," reprinted by permission of the author.

JONES, RICHARD: "The Face" from *The Correct Spelling & Exact Meaning* (Copper Canyon Press, 2010). Copyright 2010 by Richard Jones. Reprinted with the permission of The Permissions Company, Inc., on behalf of Copper Canyon Press, www.coppercanyon.org. Also published in *Image* journal and in *Bearing the Mystery: Twenty Years of IMAGE*, ed. Gregory Wolfe (William B. Eerdmans Publishing Company, 2009). "Christ in the Garden of Olives" first appeared in *Agni* journal (Vol. 82, 2015). Copyright Richard Jones. Reprinted by permission of the author.

KAMIEŃSKA, ANNA: "A Witness to Process" from *Astonishments: Selected Poems of Anna Kamieńska*. Copyright 2007 by Paweł Śpiewak. Translation and compilation copyright 2007 by Grażyna Drabik and David Curzon. Used by permission of Paraclete Press.

MARIANI, PAUL: Selected poems from *Deaths & Transfigurations: Poems* (Paraclete Press, 2005). Copyright 2005 by Paul Mariani. Used by permission of Paraclete Press.

MAJMUDAR, AMIT: "Instructions to an Artisan" from *0'0'* (Triquarterly, 2009) and reprinted in *Poetry* (June 2008). "Seventeens: Acoustics" from *Heaven and Earth* (Story Line Press, 2011). Used by permission of the author.

McCASLIN, SUSAN: "Elder Brother" first published in *Windhover* (Vol. IV: University of Mary-Hardin-Baylor, 1999), *Christianity and Literature* (Vol. 50, No. 3; Spring 2001), *At the Mercy Seat* by Susan McCaslin (Vancouver: British Columbia: Ronsdale Press, 2003), and *Imago Dei: Poems from Christianity and Literature*, ed. Jill Peláez Baumgaertner (Abilene Christian University Press, 2012). Used by permission of the author and of *Christianity and Literature*.

McNiel, Catherine: "Redemption" used by permission of the author.

Nelson: Marilyn: "The Contemplative Life" from *Faster Than Light* (Louisiana State University Press, 2013), also published in *Image* journal and in *Bearing the Mystery: Twenty Years of IMAGE*, ed. Gregory Wolfe (William B. Eerdmans Publishing Company, 2009). Copyright 2009 by Marilyn Nelson. Used by permission of Louisiana State University Press. "Cachoeira" from *The Cachoeira Tales and Other Poems* (Louisiana State University Press, 2005). Copyright 2005 by Marilyn Nelson. Used by permission of Louisiana State University Press.

Notess, Hannah: The poems "Sunday," "Thursday," "Friday," and "Sunday" were originally commissioned for Holy Week services by John Knox Presbyterian Church in Normandy Park, Washington. "Friday" appeared in the journal *Presence*. "Friday" and "Sunday" ("In the garden…") appeared in the anthology *Poems of Devotion* (Wipf and Stock, 2012), ed. Luke Hankins. Used by permission of the author and of Wipf and Stock Publishers.

Philbrick, Margaret: "Miserere" used by permission of the author.

Pratt, Mary F. C.: selected poems used by permission of the author.

Quenon, Paul: selected poems from *Unquiet Vigil: New and Selected Poems* (Paraclete Press, 2014). Copyright 2014 by Paul Quenon. Used by permission of Paraclete Press.

Rhodes, Suzanne Underwood: "Banding" from *What a Light Thing, This Stone* (Sow's Ear Press, 1999) and digitally on the BioLogos Forum (May 15, 2011). Used by permission of the author.

RUNYAN: TANYA: selected poems from *Second Sky: Poems* (Cascade Books, an imprint of Wipf and Stock Publishers, 2013). Copyright 2013 by Tanya Runyan. Used by permission of Wipf and Stock Publishers.

SAID: selected poems from *99 Psalms*, translated from the German by Mark S. Burrows (Paraclete Press, 2013). English translation copyright 2013 by Mark S. Burrows. Originally published in German as SAID, *Psalmen*, copyright 2007 Verlag C. H. Beck oHG, Munich. Used by permission of Paraclete Press.

SÁENZ, BENJAMÍN ALIRE: "New Mexico, 1992" and "Miracle in the Garden" from *Dark and Perfect Angels* (Cinco Puntos Press, 1993). Used by permission of the author. "Easter" used by permission of the author.

SERPAS, MARTHA: "As If There Were Only One" from *Côte Blanche* (Western Michigan University: New Issues Poetry & Prose, The College of Arts and Sciences, 2002). Copyright 2002 by Martha Serpas. Used by permission of the author.

SILVER, ANYA: "Ash Wednesday" previously published in *Christianity and Literature* journal, in her book *The Ninety-Third Name of God* (Louisiana State University Press, 2010), and in *Imago Dei: Poems from Christianity and Literature*, ed. Jill Peláez Baumgaertner (Abilene Christian University Press, 2012). Used by permission of the author and of *Christianity and Literature*.

SHAW, LUCI: "Bloodline" first published in *The Christian Century* journal. Selected poems from *Accompanied by Angels: Poems of the Incarnation* (Wm. B. Eerdmans Publishing Company, 2006). Use by permission of the author and of Wm. B. Eerdmans Publishing Company.

SPENCER, GREGORY: selected poems used by permission of the author.

CHIMAMANDA NGOZI ADICHIE is a widely published, award-winning author of fiction and nonfiction. Born and raised in Nigeria, she divides her time between her homeland and the United States.

AMEY VICTORIA ADKINS earned her MDiv degree from Duke Divinity School and is currently a PhD Candidate in Religion (Christian Theological Studies, Feminist Theory) at Duke University. Her dissertation analyzes colonial purity narratives tied to the Virgin Mary as theological context for questions of human trafficking and the rise of the global sex trade. She is a licensed Baptist minister and currently resides in Amsterdam, the Netherlands.

L. N. ALLEN published literary and science fiction under the name Lori Negridge Allen for many years, but the stories gradually shrunk to short shorts, then to prose poems, then to lined free verse and formal poetry. She often works with triolets as a form of meditation. Recent or upcoming poems can be found in *The Southern Review, Christianity and Literature, Connecticut River Review, Slant,* and *Art in America,* among others. http://home .earthlink.net/lorinallen285/lnallencopy/

DERRICK AUSTIN is the author of *Trouble the Water* (BOA Editions 2016). A Cave Canem fellow, he earned his MFA from the University of Michigan. His work has appeared or is forthcoming in *Best American Poetry 2015, Image, New England Review, Callaloo, Crab Orchard Review, The Paris-American, Memorious,* and other journals and anthologies. He is the Social Media Coordinator for The Offing.

JILL PELÁEZ BAUMGAERTNER is a poet, anthologist, editor, and Dean of Humanities and Theological Studies at Wheaton College in Wheaton, IL. She was a Fulbright fellow to Spain, was nominated for a Pushcart Prize, and is the winner of numerous awards. She serves as poetry editor of *The Christian Century* and is past president of the Conference on Christianity and Literature.

WENDELL BERRY is the author of more than forty books ranging from poetry, fiction, essay collections, and environmental theology. The winner of numerous awards, including Guggenheim and Rockefeller fellowships and a National Humanities Medal, he lives, writes, and farms in Kentucky. www.wendellberrybooks.com

JERICHO BROWN is an award-winning poet and associate professor in English and Creative Writing at Emory University in Atlanta, Georgia.

FREDERICK BUECHNER is a writer-theologian and the author of over thirty books ranging from novels to autobiography and sermons. A finalist for both the National Book Award and the Pulitzer, he has won many awards and been recognized by the American Academy and Institute of Arts and Letters. www.frederickbuechner.com

SCOTT CAIRNS is an author, poet, and memoirist whose works have been highly anthologized. A recipient of a Guggenheim Fellowship in 2006, he serves on the faculty of the University of Missouri.

ABIGAIL CARROLL is the author of *Three Squares: The Invention of the American Meal* (Basic Books), which was a finalist for the Zócalo Public Square Book Prize. She lives and writes in Vermont.

SUSANNA CHILDRESS is the author of two books of poetry, *Jagged with Love* and *Entering the House of Awe*. Recently, Sherman Alexie selected one of her poems for the 2015 edition of *Best American Poetry*. Childress also writes short fiction and creative nonfiction, teaches at Hope College, and makes up half of the music group Ordinary Neighbors, whose full-length CD *The Necessary Dark* is based on her writing. www.susannachildress.com

BRETT FOSTER is the author of two poetry collections, *The Garbage Eater* (Triquarterly, 2011) and *Fall Run Road* (Finishing Line Press,

2012). A new collection, *Extravagant Rescues*, is forthcoming. His writing has appeared in *Boston Review, Hudson Review, Image, Kenyon Review, Poetry Daily, Raritan, Shenandoah, Southwest Review*, and *Yale Review*. He teaches creative writing and Renaissance literature at Wheaton College.

JOHN FRY'S poems appear or are forthcoming in *West Branch, Colorado Review, Blackbird, Tupelo Quarterly*, and *Devil's Lake*, among others. He is the author of the chapbook *silt will swirl* (NewBorder, 2012). A graduate of Texas State University's MFA program, he edits poetry for *Newfound Journal* and is a PhD student at the University of Texas at Austin, where he studies medieval and early modern English literature.

EMILY GIBSON is a third generation farmer in the Pacific Northwest, harvesting words from the rich soil of faith, marriage, and family—alongside the barn chores. While keeping her eyes and heart open to the extraordinary things around her, she works as a full time family physician. She is a member of the Redbud Writers Guild. http://briarcroft.wordpress.com

DANA GIOIA is a poet and critic. He won the American Book Award in poetry in 2001. His critical collection, *Can Poetry Matter?* (1992) is often credited with reviving poetry's place in public culture. His monograph, *The Catholic Writer Today* (2014) generated an international conversation about the decline of Catholicism's presence in the contemporary arts. He has been awarded the Laetare Medal. The former Chairman of the National Endowment for the Arts, Gioia teaches at the University of Southern California.

NATHANIEL LEE HANSEN'S chapbook, *Four Seasons West of the 95$^{th}$ Meridian,* was published by Spoon River Poetry Press (2014). His work has appeared in *Prairie Gold: An Anthology of the American Heartland, Driftwood Press, Whitefish Review, The Cresset, Midwestern Gothic*, and *South Dakota Review,* among others. plainswriter.com

KATHERINE JAMES has a MFA in fiction from Columbia University where she received the Felipe P. De Alba merit fellowship. She has work published in the anthology, *In the Arms of Words* (Sherman Asher, 2005), *St. Katherine Review,* and other periodicals. One of her short stories was recently chosen as a finalist for a Narrative Spring Prize; and her novel, *Can You See Anything Now,* was a finalist for the Doris Bakwin Prize. A member of the Redbud Writers Guild, Katherine is in the process of completing a book-length essay about heroin addiction in the suburbs of Philadelphia. www.northhilldrive. com

MARCI RAE JOHNSON teaches English at Valparaiso University, where she serves as Poetry Editor for *The Cresset.* She is also the Poetry Editor for WordFarm press. Her second full length collection will be released by Steel Toe Books in 2016. http://marciraejohnson. blogspot.com/

RICHARD JONES is the author of seven books of poetry from Copper Canyon Press, including *A Perfect Time* and *The Correct Spelling & Exact Meaning.* He has won two book-of-the-year awards: the Posner Award for *Country of Air* and the Society of Midland Authors Award for *The Blessing.* He has also published five books with Adastra Press, maker of fine limited editions; his newest Adastra volume is *King of Hearts.* He is the editor of *Poetry East* and its many anthologies, including *Bliss, Origins*, and *Paris.*

AMIT MAJMUDAR is a widely published poet, novelist, and essayist. He lives in Dublin, Ohio, with his wife and three children. www. amitmajmudar.com

PAUL MARIANI is an award-winning poet, essayist, biographer, and University Professor of English at Boston College.

SUSAN MCCASLIN is a Canadian poet from British Columbia who has published thirteen volumes of poetry, including *The Disarmed Heart*

(The St. Thomas Poetry Series, 2014) and *Demeter Goes Skydiving* (University of Alberta Press, 2011), a volume short-listed for the BC Book Prize and first-place winner of the Alberta Book Publishing Award. Susan, Faculty Emeritus of Douglas College, has recently published a spiritual autobiography, *Into the Mystic: My Years with Olga* (Inanna Publications, 2014), about her relationship with the Canadian mystic Olga Park (1891–1985). www.susanmccaslin.ca

CATHERINE MCNIEL writes to open eyes to the creative and redemptive work of God in each present moment. Her Bible studies, devotions, poetry, essays, and articles can be found in various publications, and at www.catherinemcniel.com. She is a member of the Redbud Writers Guild.

HANNAH FAITH NOTESS won the Michael Waters Poetry Prize from *Southern Indiana Review*, for her poetry collection, *The Multitude* (2015). She is also the author of *Ghost House,* a chapbook of poems (2013), and *Jesus Girls: True Tales of Growing Up Female and Evangelical* (2009). She is the managing editor of Seattle Pacific University's *Response* magazine and lives in Seattle with her family. hannahnotess.com

PAUL QUENON was born in West Virginia and entered the Trappists in 1958 at the Abbey of Gethsemani in Kentucky, where Thomas Merton was his Novice Master. He has been publishing poems and photographs for the last twenty years.

MARGARET ANN PHILBRICK is an author, gardener, and teacher who desires to plant seeds in hearts. She is the author of the novel, *A Minor: A Novel of Love, Music and Memory* and a member of the Redbud Writers Guild. http://margaretphilbrick.com/

MARY F. C. PRATT has been a teacher, a parish deacon, and an apple picker. Currently, she's getting used to being a grandmother, learning to play the hurdy-gurdy, and blogging her poetry at gladerrand. wordpress.com

SUZANNE UNDERWOOD RHODES has published five books of poetry and creative prose, including her recent chapbook, *Hungry Foxes.* Her poems appear regularly in such journals as *Poetry East, Spiritus, Image, Anglican Poetry Review, Shenandoah*, and others. She is a retired college professor and an occasional instructor of poetry at the Muse Writers Center in Norfolk, Virginia. www.RhodesNotTaken. com

TANIA RUNYAN is the author of the collections *Second Sky, A Thousand Vessels, Simple Weight*, and *Delicious Air*, which won Book of the Year by the Conference on Christianity and Literature. She is also an NEA fellow, editor, private tutor, and very busy mom.

BENJAMÍN ALIRE SÁENZ is a poet, novelist, artist, and writer of children's books. His latest collection of short stories was the winner of the 2013 Pen Faulkner Award for Fiction; he is the first Hispanic to ever win that award. He teaches in the bilingual creative writing department at the University of Texas at El Paso.

MARTHA SERPAS has published three books of poems, *Côte Blanche, The Dirty Side of the Storm*, and *The Diener.* A documentary on Louisiana's vanishing wetlands features some of her work. She teaches at the University of Houston and serves as a hospital chaplain.

LUCI SHAW was born in London, England in 1928, and has lived in Australia and Canada. A poet and essayist, since 1986 she has been Writer in Residence at Regent College, Vancouver. Author of over thirty-five books of poetry and non-fiction prose, her writing has appeared in numerous literary and religious journals. In 2013 she received the tenth annual Denise Levertov Award for Creative Writing from Seattle Pacific University. Her most recent publications are *Scape: Poems* (2013), and *Adventure of Ascent: Field Notes from a Life-long Journey* (2014). She lives in Bellingham, WA. www.lucishaw.com

ANYA SILVER is the author of two books of poetry, *I Watched You Disappear* (2014) and *The Ninety-Third Name of God* (2010), both published by the Louisiana State University Press, as well as the forthcoming collection, *From Nothing* (LSU, 2016). She teaches at Mercer University and lives in Macon, Georgia with her husband and son. www.anysilverpoet.com

GREGORY SPENCER has been teaching communication studies for nearly three decades at Westmont College. He has published two novels (*The Welkening* and *Guardian of the Veil*) and more recently *Awakening the Quieter Virtues*. Among his joys are good conversations, soil in his fingernails, family laughter, and a rare forehand that reminds an undiscerning watcher of Roger Federer.

DANIEL TAYLOR (PhD, Emory University) is the author of twelve books, including *The Myth of Certainty, Letters to My Children, Tell Me A Story: The Life-Shaping Power of Our Stories, Creating a Spiritual Legacy, The Skeptical Believer: Telling Stories to Your Inner Atheist,* and a novel, *Death Comes for the Deconstructionist.* He has also worked on a number of Bible translations. www.WordTaylor. com

JEANNE MURRAY WALKER'S latest two books are *Helping the Morning: New and Selected Poems* and *The Geography of Memory: A Pilgrimage through Alzheimer's*. A Professor of English at The University of Delaware for forty years, she now teaches in the Seattle Pacific Low Residency MFA Program, and gives readings widely in this country and abroad. www.JeanneMurrayWalker.com

PAUL J. WILLIS is a professor of English at Westmont College and a former poet laureate of Santa Barbara, California. His most recent collections are *Rosing from the Dead* and *Say This Prayer into the Past.* pauljwillis.com

# NOTES

1. See *The Lion, the Witch, and the Wardrobe*.

2. Latin for a reminder that we will die.

3. Various Latin conjugations for "to love."

4. French for "old man," or sometimes "old boy" or "old friend."

5. *Comenzamos el Padre Nuestro en español*: Spanish for "We begin the Our Father in Spanish."

6. *De vez en cuando*: Spanish for "from time to time," or "occasionally."

7. *Una mancha permanente*: Spanish for "a permanent mark" or "a permanent stain."

8. Another word for mischievous fairies.

9. The good god of ancient Irish mythology.

10. From the Yoruban religion of Brazil, roughly meaning "earth and spirit."

11. A pantheon of spirits or deities in the Yoruban religion of Brazil.

12. The spirit or *Orixa* of the ocean, in the Yoruban religion.

13. A syncretic religion in Brazil.

14. Archaic past tense of "get."

15. A rallying song for the French Revolution, often accompanied by wild dancing.

16. See Psalm 49:7.

17. Latin for "O God, I love you."

18. Archaic for "began."

19. Archaic for "a great amount."

20. Archaic for "to rise up" or "ascend."

21. Archaic for "corpse."

22. Archaic for "firmament" or "heavens."

23. Noblemen whose lands were granted by a king.

24. Latin for "the rest is missing."

25. Archaic for "threefold" or "triple."

26. "Good luck" in Spanish.

27. Common fish caught in the first century, also known as St. Peter's fish.

28. Archaic for "lantern."

29. "Right" or "proper."

30. Archaic past tense and past participle of "climb."

# ABOUT PARACLETE PRESS

## Who We Are

Paraclete Press is a publisher of books, recordings, and DVDs on Christian spirituality. Our publishing represents a full expression of Christian belief and practice—from Catholic to Evangelical, from Protestant to Orthodox.

We are the publishing arm of the Community of Jesus, an ecumenical monastic community in the Benedictine tradition. As such, we are uniquely positioned in the marketplace without connection to a large corporation and with informal relationships to many branches and denominations of faith.

## What We Are Doing

### PARACLETE PRESS BOOKS

Paraclete publishes books that show the richness and depth of what it means to be Christian. Although Benedictine spirituality is at the heart of all that we do, we publish books that reflect the Christian experience across many cultures, time periods, and houses of worship. We publish books that nourish the vibrant life of the church and its people.

We have several different series, including the best-selling Paraclete Essentials and Paraclete Giants series of classic texts in contemporary English; Voices from the Monastery—men and women monastics writing about living a spiritual life today; award-winning poetry; best-selling gift books for children on the occasions of baptism and first communion; and the Active Prayer Series that brings creativity and liveliness to any life of prayer.

### MOUNT TABOR BOOKS

Paraclete's newest series, Mount Tabor Books, focuses on liturgical worship, art and art history, ecumenism, and the first millennium church, and was created in conjunction with the Mount Tabor Ecumenical Centre for Art and Spirituality in Barga, Italy.

## Paraclete Recordings

From Gregorian chant to contemporary American choral works, our recordings celebrate the best of sacred choral music composed through the centuries that create a space for heaven and earth to intersect. Paraclete Recordings is the record label representing the internationally acclaimed choir Gloriæ Dei Cantores, praised for their "rapt and fathomless spiritual intensity" by *American Record Guide*; the Gloriæ Dei Cantores Schola, specializing in the study and performance of Gregorian chant; and the other instrumental artists of the Gloriæ Dei Artes Foundation.

Paraclete Press is also privileged to be the exclusive North American distributor of the recordings of the Monastic Choir of St. Peter's Abbey in Solesmes, France, long considered to be a leading authority on Gregorian chant.

## Paraclete Video

Our DVDs offer spiritual help, healing, and biblical guidance for a broad range of life issues including grief and loss, marriage, forgiveness, facing death, bullying, addictions, Alzheimer's, and spiritual formation.

Learn more about us at our website: www.paracletepress.com or phone us toll-free at 1-800-451-5006

SCAN TO READ MORE

*Other best-selling literary guides from Sarah Arthur...*

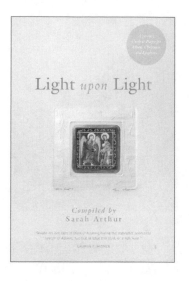

## *Light upon Light*
### *A Literary Guide to Prayer for Advent,*
### *Christmas, and Epiphany*
### Sarah Arthur

This collection of daily and weekly readings goes through the liturgical seasons of winter—including Advent, Christmas, and Epiphany. New voices such as Amit Majmudar and Scott Cairns are paired with well-loved classics by Dickens, Andersen, and Eliot.

ISBN: 978-1-61261-419-9 | $18.99 | French flap paperback

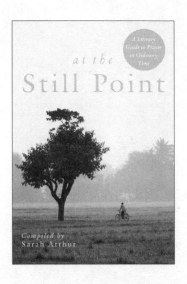

## At the Still Point
### A Literary Guide to Prayer in Ordinary Time
#### SARAH ARTHUR

This book includes classic and contemporary fiction and poetry, aimed at inviting you to experience God through your imagination during Ordinary Time. You will encounter passages from novelists from Austen and Tolstoy to Dostoevsky and Garrison Keillor and poets from George Herbert and St. John of the Cross to Scott Cairns and Kathleen Norris.

ISBN: 978-1-55725-785-7 | $16.99 | Paperback

Available from most booksellers or through Paraclete Press:
www.paracletepress.com
1-800-451-5006
Try your local bookstore first.